"Are you asking me to bite you?"

"Yes," Kim breathed. *"Please..."*

The admission seemed to tear into Stephen. Like a pouncing tiger, he slid his body up hers, stripping her tank top off and over her head. Then he pushed up her bra, tossing it away. Beneath them, the car bounced, moaning in protest.

Naked. She was naked under him, exposed and willing.

He laved one bare breast with his tongue, drawing on it as he sought her other with his hand. He smoothed his palm upward, over her collarbone, to her throat. With his thumb he circled the center of it—the tender column between her veins. He watched, as if entranced, as her pulse pounded out of control.

At Kim's startled gasp, he stirred. Moving his other hand over her backside, he slipped his fingers low, brushing against her swollen sex. At the same time Stephen nuzzled his way up her neck, where he rubbed his lips against her jugular vein.

"Do it," Kim urged. "Give me what I need...." Then she brazenly offered her neck to him. Because at this point he wouldn't, *couldn't* refuse her.

Blaze™

Dear Reader,

Vampires. They may be the last kind of hero you'd expect to find in a Harlequin Blaze novel, but when I heard there would be an EXTREME category of stories for this line, I just had to write a preternatural bad boy. After all, wouldn't a vampire be the epitome of a hot, mysterious, exciting lover?

But he had to be paired with a heroine who would balance him, and that's where Kim Wright comes in. A self-proclaimed geek, she's nonetheless sexually confident. She's also a "hunter" set to clash with Stephen Cole from the get-go. The thing is, she tracks vampires in the hopes of finding *him*—the vamp who's already bitten her once, and she wants more. However, this vampire of great experience doesn't quite remember the woman who's trying to seduce him into another bite, and that's where the trouble starts....

Have fun, and good luck with your own happy hunting!

Crystal Green

www.crystal-green.com

THE ULTIMATE BITE
Crystal Green

TORONTO • NEW YORK • LONDON
AMSTERDAM • PARIS • SYDNEY • HAMBURG
STOCKHOLM • ATHENS • TOKYO • MILAN • MADRID
PRAGUE • WARSAW • BUDAPEST • AUCKLAND

ISBN-13: 978-0-373-79338-9
ISBN-10:   0-373-79338-3

THE ULTIMATE BITE

www.eHarlequin.com

Printed in U.S.A.

ABOUT THE AUTHOR

Crystal Green lives near Las Vegas, Nevada, where she writes Harlequin Blaze novels, Silhouette Special Edition stories and vampire tales. She loves to read, overanalyze movies, practice yoga, travel and detail her obsessions on her Web page, www.crystal-green.com. She particularly enjoys writing bad vamps who're looking for redemption, just like Stephen, and if you check out her blog, you'll find that Crystal has a lot in common with Kim....

Books by Crystal Green

HARLEQUIN BLAZE

SILHOUETTE SPECIAL EDITION

Don't miss any of our special offers. Write to us at the following address for information on our newest releases.

Harlequin Reader Service
U.S.: 3010 Walden Ave., P.O. Box 1325, Buffalo, NY 14269
Canadian: P.O. Box 609, Fort Erie, Ont. L2A 5X3

To the Cornwells: Jim, Connie, Dawn and Kim—
our heroine's namesake.

A happy family makes for good reading.

1

JUST AFTER MIDNIGHT, Kimberly Wight spotted the vampire.

She absolutely knew, without a doubt, what he was. First, a number of severe blood-loss cases had been reported this past month by young women who'd frequented this nightclub, Mystique, which was located in the Marrakech Casino just off the Strip. Kim didn't have to put two and two together to reason that someone…some*thing*?… was sucking blood down at this place.

And, second, even though vampires were said to expertly blend in with the populace—that's how they survived—she recognized this one. Recognized him because her life hadn't been the same since he'd bitten her last year.

For a moment, Kim couldn't move as she watched her nameless fantasy disappear into the crowd on the dance floor, which was pulsing with colored lights that beat in time to the techno music. It was him—she knew it. Same shoulder-length, honey-hued hair tied back from the face of a dark angel. Same tall, muscled, lithe body dressed in a sharp, black, richly tailored suit and long coat.

Her body seized with heat and slight remembrance, just as it did every night when she clung to the erotic flashes of what he'd done to her. Or, at least, what she could recall of what he'd done; it was as if her brain had been made fuzzy, made unsure of what had gone on.

His whispers, summoning her to the shadows; his kisses, trailing over her forehead in tender invitation; his mouth, skimming down to her own lips as silent words stroked her mind, calming her and inviting her. And then the bite.

The Bite.

Her heartbeat flickering in wild counterpoint to the throbbing music, Kim used her elbow to nudge the man who sat next to her at the bar—her coworker. She rose from her seat, her breathing getting heavier as she continued to track the vampire's progress across the dance floor. Without losing focus, she jerked her head in the direction of a raised platform that boasted a line of white-veiled lounging beds. Young, drunk patrons, dressed in cleavage-baring tops with European labels, lounged among the silk pillows with fifteen-dollar cocktails in hand. Oblivious.

The veins in Kim's neck strummed with her gathering excitement. For the past twelve months, The Bite had consumed her. It'd been the sexiest, freakiest, most wonderful thing that'd ever happened in all her twenty-nine years. It'd shown her what she was really all about, what had been lurking under the skin of a girl who'd been all too willing to settle.

It'd also given her the courage to ask questions about what she'd always believed to be true in this world— questions that had arisen just before The Bite—when her sister had been ripped from her life.

Kim reached back to grab her partner's hand, pulling him through the dance floor's throng of undulating bodies, parting the thick cologne of their sweat.

Have to catch up…

By now, her coinvestigator from the League was yelling in her ear, battling the music. "What? You see something? What?"

Too intent on tracking, Kim avoided answering.

They jammed through the dancers, then climbed up the stairs leading to the bed platform. The white veils, lit from above, created a frothy maze. Kim guided her partner through the puzzle of shrouded mattresses.

The vampire's breath on her neck, the ache between her legs banging with slick need, his fangs piercing, entering…

"Hey!" Her partner tugged her hand, halting her, shouting to be heard. "What's got you on fire?"

She turned around to face him, a slim guy in his early twenties who worked as a computer network specialist by day. They called him Powder, but it wasn't because his skin was pale; it was because he loved skiing. The sport took up just as much of his passion as graphic-novel reading and vampire research.

"I saw one!" Kim said, her breathing thin. "We're going after him!"

"Saw…one? *Him?* Who?" Powder's brown eyes were wide. Unlike her, he'd never encountered a vampire. None of her partners at the League had. They had no idea what awaited them.

She'd never told anyone *everything* about The Bite. Somehow, the thought of sharing every detail, every treasured personal emotion, devalued the experience. In this age of instant communication and Jerry Springer tell-all, keeping something so intimate to herself made the encounter much more powerful. Of course, Kim had initially shared a PG-version of her vampire meeting with the

League—that's how she'd gotten in—but anything beyond that seemed…profane.

It might take away the magic of that night, and she couldn't deal with the loss.

"How do you know it's a vampire?" Powder added, still pulling on her hand.

She pulled Powder right back, urging him to come with her. "He's the one I…met. *The* one. Come on."

Powder, no doubt, recalled her tamed story: How this anonymous vamp had "almost bitten her" before he'd heard a sound, taken off and left her alone in the dark alley. Not quite the truth, but close enough for her comfort.

Furiously, Kim continued flipping back the bed veils as they passed each one. Not here. Not there. Just a bunch of privileged kids making out and passing out from too many drinks and drugs.

Where is he? Where could he have gone?

Powder's grip tightened in hers, and Kim knew he was about to chicken out. Even though every person who volunteered their night hours to www.vanhelsingleague.com took turns patrolling the city, hoping to catch sight of a vamp one night, he was downright afraid. None of them had ever *really* believed they would find one, had they? But the notion of earning major geek points had given each one of the five members incentive enough to patrol, whether they truly believed or not; a sighting would qualify them to post about their encounter on the Internet and gain their fifteen minutes of fame in the paranormal community.

And Kim knew about that kind of notoriety since her own sighting had given her enough credibility to write a biweekly column. The One Who Escaped—that was what everybody who posted on the message boards called her, and they read her work with adoring glee.

The League's main goal was to bring vamps into the mainstream, to prove their existence. When Kim had joined them nine months ago, it'd made sense to associate with these people who wouldn't laugh at what she'd experienced, people who would help her make sense of it all.

A support group who might be able to help her find *him* again.

But sometimes she wondered just how far the League's dedication went. Was this merely another odd club they belonged to, a fanboy pursuit as fun as their comic-book conventions or the latest X-Men movie? If they truly knew what was out there, would they be brave enough to air their pirate-radio broadcasts or maintain the Web site?

Or was it the fantasy that kept them going in life?

She didn't know the answer, because sometimes she thought that was what drove her—the fantasy of The Bite, the dream of reliving it. Ever since, she'd found nothing even close in her dating endeavors. No man matched up to The Bite; none could satisfy what the vampire had brought out in her. And she couldn't help wondering if anyone ever would.

Frustrated now, she led Powder to the last bed, inspected the two kissing girls on it, then cursed. But when she moved past the last mattress, she stopped cold at what she saw in front of her. Her belly toppled, her heartbeat slammed to a halt.

Who...

Next to her, Powder flinched, sucked in a breath. Then he laughed, pointing to the mirror where they were both gaping at their images.

"Oh, scary. Boo! Is this your vampire, Kim?"

Disbelief from one of her own. Great. That's all she needed.

The only thing that stopped her from engaging in a verbal slapdown was the sight of her own face reflected back at her.

Sometimes she still didn't recognize herself: From everyday average Kim, neighborhood bookstore clerk, to this—a vamp. But not a bloodsucking creature of the night. The Bite hadn't made her *that*. Yet…she was certainly different. More confident, willing to try anything.

The luster of heightened self-esteem had come out in her physical appearance. Her once-auburn hair, fringed by bangs and worn long and straight down her back, was now a deep flame. It was almost as if the strands were screaming, calling out for the attention she'd never gotten before and loving it. Her skin had always been redhead pale, but after The Bite, the freckles had disappeared, giving her a smooth, ivory polish. And her eyes, always a sheer blue, seemed more catlike. Five years ago, back when she lived near her parents in Tennessee, they'd always called her their Elf because of her delicate features. But now Kim thought she was more wicked creature than Santa's helper.

All because of what'd happened.

How? she wondered again. *And what am I now, exactly?*

At the questions, she urged Powder along, toward a light over a door that said EXIT. It was tucked in a corner, hidden and out of the way. Perfect for a vampire's departure.

"Hold up!" Her partner yanked her to a stop.

"What is it? Let's go, Powder!"

Her coinvestigator fumbled in a pocket, plucked out a small crucifix, then took out his cell phone. "I'm not going out there with just the two of us, even if you do have vamp experience. Haven't you learned anything from horror movies? The audience would be screaming at you right now to wait for backup!"

"Come *on!* It's not like we're out to do some slaying— we just want a peek of him on video, or his voice on tape, if either of them will even record a vamp. We won't piss him off enough to fight!" Kim's research into vampire lore indicated that the camera might not capture an image, but how did they know? It was worth a try. "That's all we're gonna do, Powder. Stealth work."

She kept her other agenda hidden. The search for another Bite.

By this time, her breasts had beaded, clearly outlined under her red tank top. Her clit had gone stiff, too, so she shifted. It rubbed against her jeans, giving her some measure of relief while at the same time exacerbating it. Slower, she shifted again, reveling in the sensation, wanting more and wondering if she'd get it.

Powder was already dialing the phone and aiming his slight body toward the restroom area, probably for some quiet. "Wait here, okay, Kim? Just wait."

As he left, she merely smiled. The League rules demanded that, on patrol, they always stick with their wingman unless going in the restroom. Just like in *Top Gun,* where Maverick learned the hard way about leaving his partner.

But this wasn't some Hollywood flick. It was real, and if she didn't start tracking again, her fantasy would disappear.

If he already hadn't.

Dammit.

As Powder walked into the crowds, Kim tapped her

booted foot, pretending to wait for him. But when he disappeared, she took off toward the exit, reaching into her pocket for the crucifix, just for insurance. She had no illusions about the danger of vampires—the severe-bloodloss cases at Mystique in the past month didn't lie. Yet, she also knew she had to do this. No doubts.

She slipped out the marked door, finding herself outside, enveloped in the June desert-night warmth. An empty painted white plaza spread out before her; on weekends, Mystique held concerts here, so there were folding chairs and bleachers facing a stage with no performer. The sight was somewhat eerie, like a rock-and-roll ghost town.

Why weren't there any kids here making out in privacy? Hell, did anyone need privacy anymore, what with those beds in the club and all?

Or had any takers just felt a niggling presence and left this area, shuddering, returning to the club's safety?

Steadily, Kim walked forward, one hand still in her back pocket to touch the crucifix. With her other, she reached into her large bag, the strap slung across her chest. Her fingers brushed against a camcorder but she ignored it, searching instead for her miniature tape recorder. Finding the device, she turned it on to capture any weird sounds.

Her heartbeat played tag with the muted thuds from the club music, and she fought to control her breathing. Sweat broke over her skin, tightening it just as evocatively as the lust riding her.

"Come out, come out, wherever you are," she said under her breath. "Where did you go?"

In answer, the air rippled. Kim froze, heart in her throat. A hushed whisper, strung along a wordless stream, flowed over the warm breeze. Untranslatable except for the anticipation heating around her.

Kim slowly turned around to where she thought the sound had originated. All that faced her was the empty stage, lit only by the faint light of the moon.

Her heart kicked at her chest. Fear. But adrenaline was making her damp, too. Damp and ready from all those nights of wanting him to come back.

Come on over to me. Sink into me again. Persuade me that my sister, Lori, never suffered and that death is beautiful....

She took a step toward the stage, but another rippling sound caught her. The vibrations dug past her skin, making the hair on her arms stand up, sending shivers all over.

Here... A sound, low and compelling, a British accent lacing words that seeped into her and drew her toward the bleachers. *Come here.*

And she did, approaching him with liquid willingness. No fear, none at all...well, maybe a little...but only enough to make the air sharpen in her lungs, the blood quicken in her veins.

Another Bite?

The shadows of the metal bleachers fell over her in slatted darkness as she came to him, obeying because she wanted to.

TIME BECAME one long pull of ecstasy. She didn't know how much of it had passed as she absorbed his sweet nothings and tender endearments. They all swirled over her, in her, through her. She had no idea what exactly he was saying, but she allowed his words to become a part of her, just as they had one year ago, mere weeks after Lori had died and Kim had still been wandering around in a numb haze. She'd been looking for meaning in every night whisper, in every step that echoed as she walked down the street. She'd found it in him.

Like every fantasy that came to her after dark, an insatiable hunger emerged right now. Her flesh breathed heat as she pieced together what she could about how he'd found her while she'd been blankly strolling to her car after a shift at The Book Bay, two blocks from her apartment in Henderson, on the outskirts of Las Vegas. He'd seduced her in this same way, hadn't he? Whispering on the air, wrapping his words around her until her limbs had gone fluid and compliant, effortlessly obeying his requests to wander over to the waiting darkness.

There, his lime-colored eyes had burned through the dim alley light. She thought she recalled him verbally stroking her with soft invitations, his caresses all but melting her clothes, her inhibitions. Hadn't he then kissed her skin, his mouth butter-warm, comforting, white-heat enlightening? Hadn't he prepared her as if he'd wanted to devour her? Then she thought he'd used his tongue to drive her to a dark and secure place she'd never gone before, an untamed cove where she'd been submerged and bathed in serenity. She thought she'd cried out, not for him to stop, but for him to go on, on, on.

Then, just as she had been on the edge of withering and breathing her last breath, he'd come into her, his fangs breaking her skin. She'd pooled into him, hot blood leaking from her, and he'd sucked her in as if she were the only thing that could ever satisfy him.

Whatever had happened—foreplay? sex?—it was all a beautiful blur except for the heady, hazy remnants. It'd left her weak, but full. So, so full. And when she'd opened her eyes to find herself splayed on the ground and propped against the wall with her clothing back on her body—a gesture she'd never comprehended—Kim had yearned for more.

Always more.

So she'd searched for it, imagining his face on every man she was with. Yet, she always ended up disappointed.

Now, she wondered if maybe he'd summoned her because he recognized her, because *he* remembered, too.

When he spoke, his voice came out of the near blackness, his body hidden. His tone swirled all around her, lethal feathers in the night.

"You wandered out here to find me."

"And you were waiting, weren't you?" Behind Kim, a pole provided the support she needed to remain standing.

"Yes, I was waiting." Now his voice was in her. "For you."

The words stroked up from her nether regions and through her belly, leaving her even damper. He *had* remembered.

All thoughts of the League and Powder's backup plan just about deserted her—just about. But in the back of her mind, she kept telling herself that vampires were dangerous, that this wasn't a game.

She scanned the area, trying to find him, then tightened her grip on her crucifix.

A flash of movement from above snagged her attention. She sucked in some oxygen, recognizing his outline against the underbelly of the bleachers. He was crouched on support beams, watching her, his long, banded hair haloed in the dim light. Gradually, the green of his gaze clarified, as if acknowledging her discovery. Burning green.

"What is your name, luv?" he asked, his foreign tone buzzing through every one of her awakened cells.

"Kimberly. Kim." It seemed as if he'd asked before, but it'd been an entire year. This time, though, she had the presence of mind to ask right back. "And yours?"

He hesitated, and she thought she heard him laugh. "Stephen."

She sunk against the pole a bit. Finally, she knew who haunted her. *Stephen.*

"So tell me, Kimberly. Why is it that there is a crucifix in your pocket?"

Startled, Kim straightened, sliding up the pole. She grasped the silver object tighter, still keeping it hidden. "A crucifix?"

"I discerned a flash of silver as you searched for me outside. Prepared, aren't you?"

Oh, had she been. "I'm a very devout girl, Stephen."

Even in the dark, she could feel, more than see, his gaze brush over her. Heavy sigh.

"Devout in what way?" he asked, voice low and knowing.

A spike of fear—a very mortal, stupid, why-am-I-doing-this-again sort of fear—thrust into her. But before she could react, he was using *that* voice on her, his eyes burning bright, tiger, tiger, in the night…

"Tell me, Kimberly. Why the crucifix?"

In spite of herself, she was manipulated into talking. "The League." She slowly blinked. "We chase vampire rumors around Vegas. This place is a paradise for creatures of the night, you know. Twenty-four-hour, everything-is-always-open opportunity. What happens here stays here, and that makes for a bunch of willing victims who find themselves doing what they normally wouldn't do at home."

"You're a…hunter?" He didn't sound panicked by that at all. Well, maybe a touch concerned, but that was it.

"More of an enthusiast."

When he shifted, the light did, too. It brought Kim that much closer to reality, even though she still felt the need to spill everything to Stephen.

Stephen.

"Why," he asked, "do you find this…investigation… necessary in life?"

Boy, his voice. It ran over her like massage oil, aromatic and soothing. It primed her.

"After my first bite," she said, knowing he knew what she was talking about, "I… Well, sometimes I wondered if I'd imagined it."

"Your first bite," he said, as if weighing the words.

Hearing him say it sent a splinter of crazed yearning through her. "There were nights when I thought I was tetched, off my rocker, that it couldn't have happened. But I *felt* the neck wound, every minute, before it healed." Healed too quickly, within a couple of days. "And the texture of it was a reminder that it *did* happen."

"And when the injury disappeared?"

"That's when I started doubting myself for real. I didn't know who to tell, who'd understand what had happened and accept it. There wasn't anybody." Not her parents, her friends, her coworkers at the bookstore. Definitely not recently departed Lori, who'd persuaded Kim to move to Vegas in the first place and then deserted her in the most permanent way imaginable.

Not her beloved older sister who'd been taken from Kim in a meaningless, split-second accident.

The thought brought Kim's confession to a halt. Her heart clenched, as if undergoing the same shock she'd felt that day when the cops had called her from the diner where

Lori had been grabbing a snack. Kim was supposed to meet her, but she'd been summoned to work early, so she'd left Lori there alone.

Yes, Kim should've been there when the car smashed through the ceiling-to-floor window where Lori had been sitting in the booth, enjoying her apple pie. Kim should've been dead, too, instead of identifying Lori's body that day.

"You're pained," Stephen said, and, suddenly, his voice wasn't as hypnotic. There was a sense of sympathy there, instead, as if he knew just what agony was.

"I got over it." The lie echoed against the bleachers.

In her bag, she touched the hidden camcorder, wondering if she should turn it on and whip it out so she could capture just a glimpse of this vampire on film. So she could keep him solid instead of a figment of her restless longing.

Then Stephen dropped down from the beams, arcing smoothly to the ground, where he crouched in the darkness. Now, the only hint of him were those green eyes.

"Tell me more about why you joined this League, Kimberly."

"I…" She shut her mouth. It seemed prudent, even in her present talky state.

Her greedy side disagreed. *Keep him here, just long enough to film him.*

But that wasn't right. Filming wasn't first and foremost on her mind: She needed to get another bite out of him. Just one more….

Would telling him about the League make him stay longer? she wondered. They weren't a big old secret black ops group or anything. All you had to do was go on the Net or listen to the radio and there they were. What harm would there be in giving him a little of what he wanted?

She went for it. "That first bite—that's why I joined the Van Helsings. Because I needed people who would understand."

There. He wasn't going *anywhere*.

"Van Helsing, named after the most famed hunter in literature." He sounded amused. "Are you a dangerous lot?"

"We've had limited luck."

With deliberate ease, Stephen stood, so tall she could feel him hovering over her, his broad shoulders coming to block the light. "But your luck is not so limited tonight, Kimberly."

To have him calling her by name was almost too much. A deep tremble nested in her belly, spreading warmth.

"This proof you seek," he said, stepping nearer, soundless in his movements, "do you realize that it could erase my existence?"

She tilted her head at him. Actually, it'd never occurred to her that a group like the League would have that sort of pull. They were a bunch of amateurs, that's all. "We're not out to kill you."

"Perhaps that's not your intention." Closer. "But this is where the persecution starts, with a few cries in the night. Then the real hunters come. That's why we do not flaunt ourselves in society, that is why we remain discreet."

"Discreet? Someone's sending women to the E.R. with a lot less blood than they started with."

Another pause. "And I'm here to put a stop to that. There is another—" He cut himself off.

Something about the way he said it poked at her. She opened her mouth to pursue it, but he moved forward quickly and came to a stop right over her so that the words caught in her throat.

His dark proximity rattled Kim, shook her until she couldn't even gasp. She wilted against the pole, trembles consuming her entire body now. He loomed, bending nearer, his aroma a mélange of leafy scents masking a predator in the night.

This was it—the culmination of all her waiting.

He sniffed at her hair, traveled lower, leaving a path of tingling heat. Kim parted her lips, drinking in the seduction, her eyelids growing as heavy and thick as the blood dragging down her limbs.

"A sweet drug," he whispered, as if remembering her scent. "That's what you…"

He stopped, honing in on something, then slipped his hand into her big purse. His skin brushed hers as he lifted out the working minirecorder. He felt cool to the touch.

Then he ran his hand over the device, crushed it to dust and casually allowed the matter to sift to the ground. Kim forced an innocent smile, thinking he had some kind of vampire night vision that would allow him to see her "oops" gesture.

A low growling emanated from his throat. "I wouldn't bother searching for any remains. What else do you have in your bag?"

At the change in his tone—from charming to scary— Kim's survival instinct took over. Her pulse raged to fight-or-flight speed, and she whipped the crucifix out of her pocket, forcing him to freeze as she backed out of the bleachers and into the moonlight. What had she been thinking? Dumb, dumb, dumb…

His growling continued as he stayed his ground, his green eyes burning at her.

"Too bad," she said, hoping to high heaven that Powder was somewhere nearby now. "I would've stuck my neck out for you, Stephen. So to speak."

With an animal flash, he forged his way forward, out of the bleachers' shadows, one arm raised. But he could go no farther once she extended that crucifix at him, emphasizing its power.

Thank goodness it worked, she thought. But why had it come to this when her wants had been so simple?

In the better light, she could see all of him. Every gorgeous, furious inch. His black coat had opened to show her a wide chest tapering to slim hips. A fallen, darkly dressed outlaw.

As they faced off, she thought she saw him smile, his fangs gleaming. But what sort of smile was it? Bitter? Respectful?

What?

A voice squealed from behind her, and she flinched. At the same time, Stephen whirled around, disappearing in a blur past the bleachers and into oblivion.

"No!" she yelled, starting to go after him.

What'd gone wrong?

But when she heard a familiar voice behind her, she knew why Stephen had left in such a hurry.

"What the hell was that?" screamed Powder. "What the friggin' hell?"

She turned around to find him wearing a panicked look, backed up by Darlene and another League investigator, Jeremy.

"That," Kim said, dropping her crucifix to her side, "was the vampire who got away, morons."

ACROSS THE TRAFFIC-CHOKED street from the Marrakech, the rogue vampire stood in a shadowed alley, watching.

His heightened vision embraced the throbbing, neon bustle before him: the casino's Arabian Nights architecture, the colored lights blazing from the roof to pierce the sky, the cars speeding up the drive to the porte cochere, the white-coated valets helping satin-swathed women and men out of their shiny vehicles.

Here, the vampire's eyesight sharpened to a point, closer, closer, until it focused on the line of one female's neck. Her throat, though decorated with gleaming jewels, palpitated under his gaze. No, no he didn't want the jewels this time, he wanted...*there*. Her jugular. Throbbing, singing in a stream of blood, just under the surface of her flesh.

His jaw stung with hunger, but it was nothing next to the need. He didn't want to sink himself into her for sustenance or pleasure so much as for another reason altogether—the same reason he had been heavily draining other women at the Mystique dance club recently. He was sending the women to hospitals and listening to the newscasts, hoping *they* would recognize what was happening and intervene.

A thin shiver traveled up the vampire, coming to outline what was once a human heart. A heart that had beat in time to mortal thoughts and ethics. A heart that had initially been designed to give out after just so many years of living.

Year by year, century by century, the vampire had come to learn that hearts—and a limited life span—were necessary. No one, not even a creature such as him, was meant to last for so long.

It was unendurable.

A keen, wonderful scent shook the vampire out of his musing. Skin, nearby.

He closed his eyes, sniffing the otherwise stale, polluted air to take in the hint of lovely blood—his savior and his curse.

When his sensitive hearing caught footsteps clicking on the alley pavement in back of him, the vampire went even stiller.

High heels, delicate and echoing against the walls.

Women walked in such a manner. Even in a surreal town such as Las Vegas, where everyone and everything was made to imitate the original, the creature could tell a born female from an impersonator.

Nearer. She was coming nearer.

The vampire opened his eyes, his vision now red with the excitement he had refused to unleash until recently, his fangs extending as the scent of her flesh—*nearer, nearer*—filtered into him. His immune system recognized the lack of disease in her smell, the purity.

Her blood—it was everything. It was the key to being saved.

Click, click, click.

As she passed, the vampire stealthily reached out of the darkness, winding her into his arms before she could scream. With one hand over her mouth, he pressed her back against him, positioned his mouth against her ear, her hair stirring as he whispered in hypnotic serenity.

You're safe. You're not afraid.

He truly wished he meant it, too.

Almost immediately, she went soft against him, her lips parting under his hand.

I'm going to make you feel good, so relax.

As she went limp, he held her, the juices flowing in his mouth as he reluctantly stroked her neck, priming her vein until it swelled, blue and neon under his preternatural gaze.

A Las Vegas sign, he thought. *And it's advertising redemption if I enter.*

Opening his mouth wider, the vampire did just that, piercing into her as she moaned in ecstasy.

2

Dawn was still a couple of hours away when the investigators made off toward "headquarters," which was basic geekspeak for where they all met every night to share rumors, study, read e-mails from the public, construct the Web site and broadcast from a highly illegal micro power station.

As Kim drove her old mint-blue Chevy into the subdivision, she sighed for the hundredth time. Powder, sitting shotgun, seemed to understand.

"We didn't mean to scare him off, Kim. Darlene and Jeremy were just on fire to see what you found, so they busted through the door and—"

"Please stop apologizing. My vamp was ready to leave, anyway. He didn't exactly love having that crucifix in his face, so things were winding down."

She said it, but she wasn't sure she meant it. Even now, miles away from the sighting, she was restless, wanting Stephen back.

Dammit, she'd been so close.

"Hee." Powder laughed. "You drew a weapon on one of them. A weapon! On a vampire! Whoo, we're just lucky the crucifix worked." He leaned his head back against the car seat. "So you think crucifixes work on all of them,

Kim? I mean, like, Anne Rice's vampires wouldn't care about that kind of thing, but Dracula—"

"Oh, Powder, those are—" Kim stopped herself. It was on the tip of her tongue to say that his examples were fiction.

But her partner actually had a good point when it came right down to it. Were all vampires the same? Did they have the same repellants? Did they all avoid sunlight?

Unable to help it, Kim also wondered if they varied in biting technique, if every single vampire took wonderful, deliberate time and left all their victims mindless sex piglets like her.

"At any rate," Powder added, "I thought I'd wait until Darlene and Jer got in their car before I said anything about this, but…"

"But, what? Spit it out."

"But Troy is gonna have a cow that you went outside alone to chase your vamp. Never leave your wing—"

"Man. Yeah, I know. But the opportunity was there and I took it."

"You lost one of our tape recorders."

Kim thought of Stephen, effortlessly destroying the running tape recorder as if it were merely crackers for soup. His decisive reaction excited her. But, then again, what didn't flip her skirt when it came to him?

She tightened her grip on the steering wheel. *Think, Kim, think. This is serious stuff. You're about to get to the bottom of everything you've wanted to know about what the vampire*—what death—*really is* and *what happened to you after that bite.*

"I'll pay for another damned recorder," she said, steering into the driveway of a black-curtained house owned by their leader, Troy. Except for the blank eyes of the windows, the building resembled each and every other dwelling on the quiet block. Beige stucco with rocks and cactus in the yard. Cookie-cutter homes, she thought, like identical grains of sand in the desert.

As she turned off the car's engine, she noted that Darlene and Jeremy had already arrived, their silver pickup parked and cooling. They were, no doubt, waiting for Kim and Powder inside. Heck, they were probably even securing front-row seats for Kim's inevitable dressing-down from Troy.

After Powder got out of the car, he slammed the door. The metallic sound reverberated through the lonely air. He seemed to read the direction of her thoughts when he said, "Good luck inside, Red."

Kim shut her own door more carefully. The Chevy was her ancient, rusting baby. "I can take Troy with one arm behind my back, so who needs luck?"

She tossed a cocky smile at her partner as he began strolling toward the house. Powder grinned back, shaking his head. He knew General Troy wasn't going to let her off easy.

When her cell phone rang, it startled her. No one but her parents would have reason to call after midnight, so she tugged the phone out of her jeans pocket. "Don't wait up for me," she told Powder. If this was a family emergency, she didn't want an audience.

Her heartbeat sped up as the phone rang again and Powder continued on his way. She glanced at the LED screen, but there was no ID. No nothing.

What?

She heard Powder close the front door before she could even flip open her phone to find that it was silent.

In that frozen second, Kim realized she was alone out here. Very alone, on a night when she'd found a vampire.

A whipping breeze pushed against her, a burst of that leafy scent she'd caught earlier back at Mystique. Before she knew it, she'd been turned around, the cell phone flying out of her hand and the dim light over the garage guttering as she slammed toward the side of her car. Dizzy, discombobulated…

A flash later, she struggled back to her senses, realizing she was pinned against the Chevy. Oddly, it occurred to her that the sudden attack should've hurt. But it hadn't.

As her vision cleared, she became aware of an arm cushioning the front of her, crushing her breasts. Then she felt a wide chest pressed against her back, and that chest was pounding like a hollow drum haunted by phantom sounds. The furious tempo beat in her own pulse.

Kim recognized the body. She'd dreamed about it so many times that she had it memorized.

A strand of hair had escaped from Stephen's low ponytail. It brushed her cheek as he leaned closer to her ear. She gasped for air, paralyzed with mounting excitement and terror.

"We have unfinished business, luv," he said softly, tickling her ear with a moist cool.

No spellbinding words from him *this* time. Nope, just a voice cut with anger.

Kim tried to swallow, but her mouth was too dry. Still, she managed to keep her composure, even though the rest of her was simmering.

"Are you here to finish it, then?" she asked, her words a brave whisper. "Did you get me alone out here by somehow manipulating my phone into ringing?"

Even while she said it, her logical side was thinking, vampires could do things like that? *Damn.*

Ignoring the question, he pressed more forcefully against her, his body hard and unforgiving. She could feel almost every contour—almost. She burned to reach back and explore him, touch him, see if he could get as turned on as she was.

Or maybe she needed therapy.

As if he could feel what she wanted, he backed off slightly, keeping his arm around her. He was still close enough that his cool presence seared her, even through her clothing.

"I would very much like to know why you and your friends are hunting me. Perhaps you'll enlighten me since I've made this special trip to your home."

"This isn't *my* place, Sherlock." She was starting to pant. "I told you. We're harmless."

"And I recall telling *you* that your group is not. Now, luv, stand and deliver for me."

The phrase hit a pleasure button. It was demanding, like a bandit intent on stealing valuables.

With a shock, Kim realized that she *wanted* him to order her around like this; no other man had ever dared with her. Why? Well, before The Bite, she'd dated polite guys and rarely had sex with them. Afterward, she probably came off as too self-assured for her more aggressive dates to even try. Didn't any of them think she'd react well to commands?

Maybe she scared regular men now. Was that her problem?

As she listened to him breathing softly behind her, she thought that it didn't matter, because Stephen wasn't *any* man. Not by any stretch of the imagination....

Her legs went rubbery, but he stabilized her, effortlessly maneuvering her over to the car's hood so she could keep herself standing. Even now his arm was wrapped around her, squashing her sensitized breasts. Maybe he thought she was going to run.

If only he knew.

"Stand and deliver?" she asked, daring to continue the ragged thread of their conversation. "What are you going to take from me besides information, Stephen? What do you want?"

For emphasis, she shifted, skimming her breasts against the inside of his forearm, almost groaning with the friction.

He paused as if struck. She wasn't sure if vampires cared as much about sex as blood, but she was going to do everything and anything to get what she wanted.

Slowly, Kim moved so that one of her breasts smoothed into Stephen's palm. *Oh.* At the same time, she pushed backward in a sly taunt, pressing her ass against his lower thighs. She rubbed, catlike, luxuriously and confidently.

"Tell me what you want," she repeated, hoping for the right response.

Breath quickening, he sheared his fingers over her breast, shaping her hardening nipple. Kim winced, lowering her head and biting her lip to keep from making a big noise. He slipped his fingers under the fullness of her, exploring, then cupping her in his palm, a sinuous action that sent a whisk of electricity into her clit.

Maybe he can't help himself, Kim thought. *Just like me.*

Dazzled, she rubbed her derriere against him again, encouraging him.

With a tight groan, he slid his other hand over her ass, mapping her cheeks and seeming to forget about his original request for information.

Oh, *good*. Kim rested over the car's hood because her legs just couldn't hold her up anymore. "Take what you want. I dare you, Stephen. Just take it."

"I see," he said, tone rough yet somehow controlled. "You're one of those women who loves The Bite. I've heard about your kind. You've experienced it once and it wasn't enough."

A burst of desire lit her up, making her throb and ache with wet yearning.

It was happening, and she could barely take it. Her belly clenched so violently she thought she might climax before anything really started. But Stephen was the one responsible for bringing this frantic need out in her; he'd been the one who'd coaxed the primal cat that clawed and scratched, that hunted on her own terms until she'd found what she desired. This was all his doing.

When he guided a hand under her tank top to her stomach, the coolness of his touch made her muscles leap. As he skimmed her belly ring, she heard him laugh softly. He traced patterns lower, fingers like brands.

Shaking, Kim laid her cheek on the car's hood, skin slick against the paintjob. Weak, she was so weak she could barely move.

He eased his palm upward, over her bra and higher, until he inserted his fingers into the cup of it to tease her nipple. In a strangled whisper, he asked, "Tell me your impression of the first bite, Kimberly."

It was as if he'd poured syrup over her—melting, warm, sticky. She felt composed of it.

"I… Oh…" She bit her lip as he rolled her nipple between his thumb and index finger. "I can't really remember."

He laughed again, low and soft. "That hardly sounds delightful."

"Oh, it was." She moved her hips, inching back until she found his thighs again. Hard. Was the rest of him the same way? "It was the best thing that ever happened to me, even if most of it was a fog. But I know it—"

He'd stroked his other hand between her legs, his long fingers massaging through her jeans. "You know it was what, luv?"

She moaned, losing herself. "I know it was amazing. I wanted it to happen again and again."

"Would you like me to bite you? Is that what you're asking for?"

She reached down to his hand, pressing it against her sex with wanton greed and moving her hips in time to their rhythm. Heavy, she was so heavy there, like a thick layer of expandable matter holding in a flood of liquid.

"Yes," she breathed, "bite."

Grinding against his hand, she closed her eyes, hurtling toward a mental bank of bright bulbs. Her brain had almost completely shut down, a slave to the rest of her body.

He lifted her to the hood, gently yet firmly flipping her over until she faced the night. He did it with such easy strength that it sent a spatter of tightness through her. But she wasn't ready to finish yet.

She started to unzip her jeans, needing the freedom.

Her gaze focused on him—dark, hovering, demanding Stephen—and everything locked into place for a buzzing moment. His eyes were blazing, as if undressing her with the heat. She felt her body drain, not of blood, but of something else, as if he were feeding just the same.

His intensity washed flame over every inch of her skin, and she fumbled with her fly. He helped her, his hands cool and assured as he slipped her jeans down her hips. Then, almost casually, he stroked between her legs, every movement whisking her slick lace panties against her sex.

He watched, a sense of wonder on his otherwise still face. "Your pulse. I can feel it everywhere. Here…" He pressed against her clit, making her legs spread wider as she groaned. "And—" he raised his chin, as if sensing the air around them "—everywhere."

Then, he halted all movement, as if tuning in to some unheard sound. Kim protested but, seconds later, she caught the faint putter of a car's engine fading into nowhere. Her skin flushed as she realized that she was splayed over her car's hood in front of sky and country with a vampire strumming her to a finale. What if Powder came back out? What if…

Ah, so what?

With the car gone, she wiggled her hips, inviting him to continue. He did, resuming his erotic petting by tracing the folds of her sex with his thumb, making her flesh plump with more blood and sensitive need.

"When?" she asked, not knowing how much longer she could stand it.

A rakish smile lit by moonlight made him look both trustworthy and deadly at the same time. A peak of emerged fang did a lot to accomplish that last part.

Her heart stuttered. This was real. This was happening.

"Aren't you bold," he whispered. "Usually, when I hunger, I don't trouble myself with such difficult donors."

"But you're hungry now, aren't you? You're—"

Before she could finish, he divested her of boots, jeans

and panties. It happened in a heartbeat. The next thing she knew, he'd parted her legs even wider.

The night air breathed against her, and she pulsated at the vulnerable state she was in. And, when he spread her lips open with his fingers, her clit was suddenly painful, begging for him.

Fangs, she thought too late as he lowered his head to her. *What if he...*

He licked upward, coating her slit with his tongue. She slid her body up the car's hood, crying under her breath while moving with him.

Pausing, he watched from between her legs, his eyes a devilish green. "Are you afraid?" His murmur was hot, ruffling the thatch of hair covering her mons.

Kim swallowed past the lump in her throat. "Yes."

"Do you think I'll hurt you?"

"I don't know."

Something foreign seemed to dim his gaze for a fleeting second. But then, he lowered his head again, using his tongue to tease her. Kim arched up, crazed, her hands clutching windshield wipers, snapping one of them clean off.

Clearly stoked by her response, he buried his face in her, lapping, kissing, thoroughly working her until she was gyrating and grinding her teeth.

Fangs. The thought resurfaced. *What about his fangs?*

Then, she felt a scratch.

Horrified, electrified, she yelped. But then he thrust his tongue inside of her, mining her with the deepest kiss possible, swirling and sucking and turning her into a vortex.

"Damn you," she said, jamming the loose windshield wiper against the car. "Damn you for doing this to me."

The words seemed to tear into him. Like a pouncing thing, he disengaged from her sex and slid his body up hers, stripping her tank top off and over her head at the same time with otherworldly, fluid movements. Then, his eyes that same bright green, he pushed off her bra, tossing it away. Below them, the car bounced, moaning in protest.

Naked. She was naked under him, exposed and willing, stimulated and drenched with an approaching orgasm.

As if to second that, a more intense tightness coiled in her belly, ready to spring at the right provocation.

He laved his tongue around one bare breast, drawing on it as she buried her hands in his long hair, tugging off the leather band that held it back. The soft strands went spilling down over her forearms, flirting with her own skin. In her heightened state of arousal, she caught the scent of honey, of foliage that shielded bright eyes in the night.

Again, he scraped her flesh, and she hitched in a startled breath.

"Kimberly," he said—or maybe he didn't say it. Maybe it was in her mind, in her every thought.

Sucking her breast, he sought her other with his hand, then smoothed his palm upward, over her collarbone, to her throat. With his thumb, he circled the center of it—the tender column between her veins.

His other hand eased under her, over the curve of her ass. He squeezed, his fingers lowering between her cheeks to brush her swollen sex.

How much longer?

Little by little, the tightness in her belly stretched, ready to break. It was like waiting for a snake to strike, and Kim knew she should get out of its way, but she didn't want to. She wanted the pain, the delight, the poison.

Stephen finally nuzzled his way up to her neck, where he rubbed his lips against a jugular vein. It throbbed in demented time, her blood speeding through her body.

"Do it," she urged. "Give it."

He tilted his head until he was looking at Kim, and what she saw frightened her, delivered her.

The need in his gaze... She knew, at this moment, that if she were to change her mind, it would all but kill him. Kim had become his everything, just like the first time. She recalled it clearly now—how could she have forgotten?

High on that realization, she led his mouth back to her neck, brazenly offering it.

His body went rigid, and he raised his head, then came into her.

Kim groaned, stunned by the pop of fang into skin. It was agonizing, but only for a second. After that, as he entered her completely, she felt full of him, engorged while she fed off his passion for her. Then came the vein-heavy feeling that it would all be okay in the end, that she shouldn't fear dancing this close to death.

They moved together, body to body, as he sucked. She felt energy draining from her. Dizzy, so dizzy. Yet, simultaneously, she was getting stronger, a flash force building within her with such power that she was swept away in its embrace.

Wave...upon wave... Higher...

As she reached the sky's night ceiling, the point of a star pierced her skin. Then another. Another. They entered her until she was full of holes yet charged by their light. She flared, the buzz pressing outward, against the shell of her body—

Then she burst, a supernova sparking blood. She rode

the crimson wave down, floating, weakening, until she was back in her body, cradling Stephen, who shuddered, then panted against the skin of her throat. He was caressing the side of her neck, her bruised and sticky wound, as if wanting to heal her.

She couldn't say anything. He didn't speak, either. But when the fire finally began to slip out of her and into the air, leaving her calmer, she tested her voice.

"This," she said, croaking with emotion, "was maybe even better than the first time."

He lifted his head to look at her, and what she saw by moonlight on his face gave her a jolt. But not a good one. Not a good one at all.

Something like confusion was dimming his gaze.

Then it hit her.

"Crap," she said, her heart taking a dive. "You don't remember biting me the first time, do you?"

3

HE HAD BITTEN her before?

As the woman, Kimberly, fixed a brutally bewildered gaze on Stephen, he instinctively shut out the flood of unidentifiable fulfillment still thrashing through him and glanced away. He came to stare at the car's windshield, where the moon was reflected in wan apathy. Stephen's own image was nowhere to be seen in the glass because, unlike the moon, nothing cared to reflect him. He was *vampyr.*

Truly, he had bitten her before?

Stephen searched his memory, but there had been so many women throughout the ages. Perhaps, when he was a younger creature, he might have recalled a feeding from only a year ago. But now his days faded together, indistinguishable, just as many of the world's cities were becoming. Homogenized, McDonald's-ized, a progressive blur.

Yet, to his knowledge, he had never bitten anyone twice, though, he was not surprised it had happened. His existence was so rote that he did not pay attention to the details of victims anymore. All the same, his apathy was required. Long ago, he had decided that allowing someone to move him was destructive: the world around Stephen was fleeting, speeding past in the blink of an eye. More than 130 years ago, he had learned the hard way how foolish attachment was, with a woman who had ultimately found him repulsive. She had gone on to fall in love with a mortal, marry, to be happy and had succumbed to a peaceful death.

However, unlike humans, a vampire's pain never died.

Despite this, Stephen occasionally found himself yearning to look forward to something... Anything... *Anyone.*

Now, his predatory vision allowed a peripheral scan of this woman he had chosen tonight in his blinding hunger. He had been so consumed with family matters lately that he had delayed feeding; hence, tonight, it had been all too simple to lose control and succumb to his ravenous urges.

Kimberly. Hair like blood rain, eyes clear and tempting, a smile that shined with confident invitation; A hunter who had gotten the best of him earlier. At first, he had found it charming that she had called herself a "hunter," yet he had found the situation less so when she had mentioned the drainings that the rogue had been performing.

Out of extreme concern, he had tracked her to this house, determined to secure more information about who she was, what she knew and why she wanted to record his voice and image. These hunters could present infinite danger to Stephen and his vampire family, perhaps even compounding the crimes of this rogue creature he had been assigned to hunt—an unknown criminal who was draining women and threatening to expose the vampire kind with all his mindless bloodletting.

Yes, investigating *her* as much as he was investigating *him* was important. After Stephen discovered what this Kimberly and her hunter group already knew about the rogue and about vampires in general, he could stop the Van Helsings from spreading the truth about their existence. He could stop them from destroying a vampire's best means of survival—secrecy.

As well, it might even be possible that these hunters knew something about the rogue that could help Stephen in his quest.

As his family's enforcer, it was his duty to keep his brethren safe. It was necessary and right. He would do anything to succeed.

He had merely been distracted tonight.

Even now, he could still taste her on his tongue, and a quiver spiraled through him. Her blood was not the only sustenance that had filled him tonight, there was something else, as well, a force he had drawn from her frank sexuality. A disturbing new aphrodisiac that was upsetting his normally calm balance.

Stephen fought off the urge to look at her again, but he could not put her out of his mind. Twice bitten? How?

Was it because of her scent, her blood? A puzzling concoction: Primitive, yet clean and innocent. An opiate he *should* have recalled imbibing before.

Had he become so immune that he could not relive pleasured memories?

"How…" Kimberly asked softly, sounding so hurt that it pricked his very skin. She was shaking, most likely due to her blood loss. "How could you not remember that bite?"

Though she spoke with passion, he knew that she couldn't recall every detail of their previous encounter He never allowed mortals the chance to grasp the particulars—it was a point of survival. So how could it have affected her all that much? And why?

Stephen reached for her jeans, holding them toward her so she might warm herself. Still a gentleman, he thought, and always the scoundrel who left his victims with the dressed feel of dignity after he had gotten what he needed from them.

Oddly, she refused to take the material.

A baked breeze jostled past him, air tinged with the presence of nocturnal creatures and suburban life: Grease from an outside grill nearby, the anonymous blandness of the desert's scalding vigil.

Remain unaffected, he told himself. *Don't attach, because you know the price.*

He donned a careless smile, gradually moving away from her while shielding himself from the impact of her disappointment. "I am a vampire of great experience, luv. Forgive me if I don't recall a past bite."

"Forgive you?" She clenched her jaw to shut off more words, her gaze wide and glassy. At that moment, she seemed to realize that she was still holding the windshield wiper she had torn off during a fit of ecstasy. She threw it to the ground.

Stephen blocked the reminder of their interlude. He did not care to dwell on the weakness she had brought out in him. "Don't take it personally. You drew me with your beauty, and I responded as any self-respecting vampire would."

He refrained from adding that *all* his victims were lovely, and this was probably the reason he had chosen to bite her one year ago. It had no doubt happened during one of his reluctant visits to Vegas in order to find food, which he required merely once every two weeks, these days. Stephen preferred the blood of attractive women; their aesthetic value lured him and ultimately offered a facsimile of the passion he never allowed himself to experience. Every bite provided not only sustenance, but a giddy rush, a temporary glimpse of what it might be like to feel once more.

"Oh, I see," Kimberly said, her tone laced with what Stephen perceived to be sarcasm, "it's all about *beauty.* You know, you should really check out the Miss America pageant when it comes back to town. It'd be a regular orgy for you."

Anger. Her emotion scratched at Stephen. "I don't intend any disrespect. Sharing your blood was…"

He lost the ability to describe, oddly tongue-tied as the experience reawakened within him. The complete, thick taste of her, the cataclysmic delight of taking her in.

Stephen hardened himself further. This woman had been no different from the others and, after tonight, she would be forgotten in a miasma of more victims. She meant nothing to Stephen. She could not.

From where she sat on the car's hood, Kimberly continued to level a crushed glare at him. She seemed too bothered to note that her body was bared. More precisely, her vulnerability was beneath the flesh, where she could not cover it.

Gathering composure by the moment, Stephen tried not to visually caress her from head to toe, to imagine drinking in every inch of skin in order to retain her essence.

She caught his perusal and brightened, as if he had somehow relayed his remorse. Then, quite naturally, she grinned, leaned back against the windshield with her arm over her head. A sigh of pure relief accompanied the gesture. It was as if he had given her a reprieve from the wounding reminder that he hadn't remembered their first bite.

For some reason, he liked her resilience, but he knew his appreciation couldn't last.

Moonlight stroked her skin, paling it, making the blood-bright wound at her neck stand out; it had begun to heal due to his touch. Her full breasts, tipped with large, dark nipples, urged him to latch his mouth on their ripeness again, creating bites and wounds there, as well.

Stephen glanced away, not trusting himself.

"What?" she asked, her voice losing its strength. "Have you already forgotten how good *this* bite was? It was better than any sex I've ever had. Slow, orgasmic, mind-blowing... Do all you vampires bite like that?"

She was baiting him, and he was fool enough to almost give in. Time to stop this nonsense. "I'm not always so deliberate, Kimberly. In fact, there are times when I strike for blood, when I drain my victims merely because I need to survive or merely because it feels good."

Suddenly, all her playfulness evaporated. At the mention of draining, her splayed arm fell forward to cover her chest. He was not certain if she had returned to looking so devastated because of the recent victims from Mystique or because he had reinforced that she was only another bite to him.

"So you *are* the vamp who's been going around putting women in the E.R.?" she asked.

"No." Now was the time for him to pursue a far better reason to have followed her to this house. A reason beyond hunger.

He reached out with his mind and attempted to *peek* into hers, to see what she really knew of the rogue.

Slam!

A mental block, a wall? Why could he not see into her?

In the near distance, Stephen discerned the click of a door opening—the front door of this house.

With a regretful whir of speed that a human eye could never translate, he slipped her clothing back over her form, careful not to touch her intimately lest he be tempted to sweep her off and enjoy her some more. Then he softly laid his fingers against her temple, leaving her memory fuzzy. It also served to infuse her with a sense of false energy so she wouldn't appear overly weak to herself or others, at least at first. He had sipped his fill tonight, enough to be satisfied, but he didn't want it to be obvious.

Without even a farewell, he speared upward, flying away before anyone else could discover him.

Yet, as he traversed the sky on the short trip back to his family's hideout, he knew that he and Kimberly still had unfinished business and that he would be back to see what these hunters knew.

IT WAS AS IF Kim had wandered through an electrical storm.

As the light over the garage dimmed back on, she lay sizzling in the aftermath of Stephen's presence, wondering what the hell had just happened.

Literally.

She shook her head of its haze. She knew she'd been bitten again, and that Stephen had turned her world into one fierce orgasm, but she wasn't sure of the details.

Except for one, and she wished she could dismiss it. He hadn't remembered the defining moment of her life. And in that instant of revelation, he'd stripped her of everything she thought she knew about herself. In the end, she felt a sense of shame, puzzlement...rejection. Then he'd flown off in a blur, leaving her alone, flailing.

Or...

He'd flown off, right? He'd actually been here?

Reeling, Kim sat up from the windshield and glanced down at her body. She was fully clothed. What…

Oh, my God. It couldn't have just been a fantasy. She couldn't have imagined it.

All her worst fears crowded in on her: all the worries about people not believing what she'd gone through one year ago. Had Kim wanted Stephen so badly again that she'd made this latest visit up? Was she losing it?

She heard the house's door open, and she sprang up from the car's hood, blood pumping, though she wasn't sure why. Then a wave of dizziness forced her to lean against the car near the mirror.

Loss of blood? She wondered how pale she looked, how fatigued she might get. Orange juice, she needed some orange juice and food right away.

Then again, as she touched her clothing, her doubts about being bitten returned.

That's when she felt the crusting soreness on her neck, a tenderness. Laying a hand there, she sucked in a sharp breath. Puncture wounds. It *had* happened, dammit. *Yes!*

She heard footsteps, then Powder's voice. "Kim? You done with your phone call yet? I waited and waited, but something told me to stay inside. Don't kill me for intruding if—"

She wondered if Stephen had used his powers—hypnosis?—to keep everyone away temporarily. "It's okay, Powder."

Expediently, she checked her clothing, then the side mirror on the car to see if her slightly paler-than-normal skin held any trace of blood. She found none. Stephen had been meticulous.

Quickly, she shoved her long hair over her shoulder to

one side, masking the bite. Good God, even if she had a scarf or something to cover it up, it was too hot for that kind of fashion nonsense. Besides, she never wore scarves. Fashion no-no, uh-uh, never.

But she wasn't about to share this second bite—heck, not even this latest sighting—with Powder. Like the first, it was hers to keep; the only things she really had to call her own.

She was bent down to retrieve her phone from the ground. Still in working order. She got up, but a wave of dizziness tumbled over her and she leaned against the car for balance.

Then Powder appeared around the walkway corner in all his lanky glory. He was holding a crucifix out in front of him like a nauseated infantryman on the march with his first gun.

"You can put that thing away," Kim said, trying to seem casual as she tucked her phone into a jeans pocket. While she opened the car door to retrieve her bag, the disappointment hit her once more. She'd been so excited about the reality of this second bite that she'd almost forgotten the aftermath again, the sickening drop of her stomach in confusion because Stephen hadn't remembered her.

She hadn't rocked his world at all—not like he'd rocked hers. It was like being the wallflower in high school and finding out that you'd been elected prom queen, then revelling in the happiness of knowing that people thought you were one way when you'd always believed you were another. But then…oh, God, then the principal announced over the loudspeaker that they'd miscounted the votes and you were the loser; still the wallflower who'd never blossomed into something more.

Had her sexual confidence all been a lie? Had she only created it out of a desperate need to connect with someone? Were all the men she'd been with secretly laughing behind her back after she'd gone home because she'd made an ass of herself by acting sexier than she really was?

After Kim shut the car door, she took a step toward Powder, but it felt as if the bottom had fallen out of her world. She stumbled.

Powder sprinted forward to help, flashing his crucifix around him at the same time in total fear. He looped her arm over his shoulders, acting as a crutch. "Kim?"

"I, uh…" Think fast. "It was a bad-news call. My parents had to take the family dog in to the vet and they wanted me to know. I spent a lot of good years with Roofer."

She almost cringed at the lie while Powder helped her to the door. As they approached, the black curtains that kept prying eyes from peeking through the windows seemed to stare accusingly. Kim only hoped Roofer would forgive her this little falsehood, bless his old dog heart.

"That sucks," Powder said, opening the door and leading her inside. He seemed relieved that he hadn't needed to use the crucifix to save her or anything.

He shut the door, allowing the sounds of controlled chaos to rule: Voices from the first bedroom in the hallway, where the crew would be preparing to go on the air with a broadcast; the squawking of police scanners; the droning of a late-night movie from the family room TV. After letting go of Powder, Kim stood on her own, thanking him as he headed in the direction of the radio equipment. Then she sank to the floor, resting a minute, planning how to get out of here so she could go home and tend the wound before it was discovered.

She didn't know how long she lollygagged, sitting there and pretending to go through her shoulder bag in case one of her partners happened by, but eventually she made her way to the kitchen, where Jeremy intercepted her. He was a spike-haired high-school senior, over six feet, a bench-warming offensive lineman who liked reading more than blocking. Black-framed glasses perched on his nose and, though they weren't held together by tape, they did have a certain nerdy vibe to them. That, and the fanboy comic T-shirts he favored, marked him as prime Van Helsing material.

"Troy wants to see you," he said in his bass monotone.

Feeling dizzy again, Kim was careful to keep her bite side away from her coworker's view as she opened the fridge. In finer form, she could probably think of a thousand smart comebacks to have Jeremy take back to Troy, but she wasn't in the mood. Somehow, knowing that she was so forgettable to Stephen sapped her of all verve.

You thought he made you into a woman or something? she asked herself. *Yeah, your rite of passage seems to be a complete failure, Kim. What a sex goddess you turned out to be.*

Jeremy, who was a pretty sensitive guy, responded to her silence by leaving the kitchen. "I'll tell him you're coming."

Yeesh. She uncapped an orange juice and drank straight from the bottle, not giving a fig about messiness.

Shame pervaded her, and she felt like sinking into the ground. If she was confused about what The Bite had made her before, now she had an answer. Nothing. She was nothing. And maybe all there was to this world was nothing.

Shutting the fridge door, she carried the juice with her,

tucking her hair in place again and tracing a hand along the bare walls just in case she stumbled.

I am a vampire of great experience, luv. It came to her out of the misty blue of her confusion. *Forgive me if I don't recall a past bite.*

She obviously had enough blood in her system to blush—yeah, actually *blush*—because she could feel the embarrassed heat coating her skin as she entered the first bedroom. There, Troy, Jeremy and Powder were fiddling with some kind of amp in their little pirate power station. They had everything—players, mixers, a transmitter and antenna, filters, compressors, computers. Kim couldn't name everything and, frankly, she didn't care. Electronics weren't her joy.

Troy wore headphones—one ear covered, one not— over his golden hair. He was a good-looking guy who shouldn't have been a geek, but his out-of-control love for the esoteric prevented that. He dug chess, science, computers, movies and Marvel—every one of them the kiss of death for a male struggling to get dates in the real world. At his day job as a corporate lawyer, he was even known to have a framed picture of Buffy the Vampire Slayer on his desk. Most girls probably weren't sure what to make of him, although, he reportedly did okay in that department. Kim herself thought he was too sweet to seduce, even if the thought had crossed her mind once or twice.

But sex in the workplace, much less the tight-knit League, was never a good idea. "Don't poo where you get your grub," Lori would've told her.

More sadness piled onto what Kim was already feeling. It was the icing on her cake of rejection.

Seeing her, Troy stood straight, hands on hips, dark blue eyes frosty. "What the hell, Kim?"

She had no gumption to get lippy about what she'd done at Mystique earlier. She merely made a bring-it-on motion with her hand while putting on a decidedly blasé expression.

"Listen," he said, his cheeks getting two little pink spots on them, "we've got rules for a reason. You could get hurt."

While wiring something or other, Powder nodded seriously. Jeremy just futzed around with the computer, blushing for her.

"I know the rest," Kim said halfheartedly. "My ego's writing checks my body can't cash. And if I don't shape up, I'm going to find myself flying a cargo plane full of rubber dog shit out of Hong Kong."

Jeremy and Powder cracked up at the *Top Gun* quotes. Troy wasn't quite as amused.

For Kim's part, discovering that she could still toss out a decent joke, even in the clutches of depression, was a bit of a boon.

Well, at least it *should've* bucked her up, but when the bite on her neck began pulsing, she wanted to cry. Was it because it had the power to turn her on again?

Troy was shaking his head, knowing his chiding was fruitless. "I'm about to go on the air, so I'll give you a complete butt-chewing later. But I don't want you to end up like one of those women in the E.R."

At her blank stare, he turned back to Powder, who looked away from Kim quickly, too. Troy had been the one who'd gotten the information about the blood-loss victims from the hospital—he knew someone who knew someone else who had the scoop. But Kim realized the so-called epidemic bothered him on a profound level, because it was evidence of the vampires they talked about on the radio and the Web site. It meant they were that much closer to actually getting proof.

But, when they found it, how would they react? How would these fanboys deal with a face-to-face encounter?

With the boys off her back, Kim left the room, drinking more OJ. She should get right on the computer to file a report about what had happened to her tonight, and she knew Troy would want to interview her on the air, but for the first time since joining, she didn't want to be here. She needed to get sleep, to think through what'd happened, to decide what to do next.

"Pssst!"

The sound stopped Kim, and she backtracked to the third bedroom, across the hall from the first. Inside, near the guest bed and at a spartan desk, she found the only other girl in the League, Darlene, tapping away at a laptop computer. She was probably answering excitable message-board postings from people responding to the general sighting headline on their Web site.

"You get busted?" Darlene whispered, dark eyes wide. Her parents were Portuguese, and they'd bequeathed her a head of dark brown, very curly hair that she usually wore in a low bun at the nape of her neck. She had a fine nose and olive skin, never wore makeup and never went out of her apartment except to come here and go to work at the preschool where she taught each weekday.

"I haven't gotten punished yet, but the wrath of Troy is considerable." Kim stood on Darlene's left side, sheltering Stephen's bite from her coworker. She took another gulp of juice. "I'm on the bad list right now."

"Oh, right." Darlene faced Kim. "Those boys worship you, just as much as your readers do. You're, like, the queen of us."

Dammit, Darlene knew these types of conversations were mortifying to Kim. The other woman always maintained that Kim was like the cool girl in school—the pretty one who all the boys secretly liked—who didn't think anything about hanging out with the nerds at lunch to discuss the latest *Alien* movie or whatever. And while the nerds freaked out at her presence, she didn't notice the ruckus she was causing.

"Yeah, yeah. Anyway…" Kim began.

Darlene rolled her eyes, cutting off the protestations. But when she peered at her friend again, she narrowed her gaze. "You look like flying pigeon turd, girl. You okay?"

"Me? Yeah."

"Duh. Listen to me, of course you're not okay. You ran into your vamp. That must've been a shock."

Although Kim had given Darlene, Jeremy and Powder an abbreviated version of the Mystique encounter when they'd shown up at the club, she wanted to tell Darlene more—about the first bite, the second, what each had done to pump up her confidence or destroy it. She needed to talk to someone, and her coworkers at The Book Bay wouldn't cut it. What helped was that Darlene was the only person who had any inkling whatsoever of how important Kim's first vamp encounter had been to her, since Kim had told her friend a little more than she'd told the guys.

But not much more.

Ultimately, she settled on *kind of* talking about it, without mentioning the all-too-intimate bites themselves. "Believe it or not, the vamp didn't…remember me, Darlene. Not at all."

Her coworker frowned.

"I mean, he…visited me and when I reminded him that he'd…paid me a call before, he'd forgotten. Just…*bloop*… forgot about it." The shame came back, and it stirred her defensive anger.

Across the hall, Troy's voice went into broadcast mode—hurried, yet low and persuasive.

Darlene got up to shut the bedroom door while Kim sat on the paisley bedspread of the guestroom mattress. She lay down, suddenly more tired. The black curtains over the window gave a bleak slant to the walls, which were decorated with framed prints of *Firefly* characters.

"The thing is," Kim said, almost whispering, "and this sounds crazy, but meeting that vampire was a big moment in my life, Dar. It…shaped me and made me think that I'd finally found out what I was about. It made me feel kind of…"

"Special?"

"Exactly."

The other woman shook her head. "Wow, I understand. It makes you more than a number in a world of digits. It's almost like a guy forgetting that he's made a pass at you."

Or forgetting that he'd *slept* with you. Oh, too humiliating to even admit.

"I'm forgettable," Kim added.

Darlene rolled her eyes again, but Kim knew it was true. She was a bad bite, which had to be akin to being a bad lay. Her ego smoldered in the ashes of this realization.

"Forgettable, my patootie." Darlene laughed. "If this were a normal guy, I'd tell you to just go back out there and hunt the weenie down. Make yourself *un*forgettable, know what I mean? Besides—" Darlene gave a little squeak "—he's a *vampire,* Kim. What I'd give to be in your place, meeting the same hot one, twice."

Kim blinked. Whoa. Darlene had no idea what she'd just suggested…or how much sense it made to a woman who'd just lost all self-esteem. True, Darlene's advice was twisted and ridiculous, but…

No, it was too impulsive, too dangerous.

But if she *could* become the ultimate bite for the vampire who'd captured her imagination, who'd ruled her life, would that make her feel better? Would proving to him that she wasn't a nobody bring back the old oomph?

The wound on her neck began beating, flashing out a naughty cadence. It was a lame idea, setting out to seduce a vampire but, Lord help her, it made her feel good again. She *was* somebody, or else…

Or else she was as good as dead to him—just as blank as her sister, who'd never had a second chance to resurrect herself.

Struggling to stand—she wanted to cover the wound with something in the bathroom cupboards—Kim patted Darlene on the back while moving toward the door.

"Thanks for the talk," she said, fighting off the sadness that thoughts of her sister always brought.

But, as she entered the hallway, a reckless compulsion stole into her like a shadow inching over a threshold. A shadow that kept whispering for her to invite it all the way inside, where it would complete her.

Where it would truly make her the woman she *thought* she'd become.

4

STEPHEN HAD FLOWN straightaway to his home, his family, his only shelter. He escaped from the devastated look on Kimberly's face while regret grew like a rip in his chest.

Surprising, that.

He tried to tell himself that the regret was born only of his failure to extract any useful information about this Van Helsing League from her, yet he knew there was more. There was something dormant that she had touched and awakened, something that had remained so long buried that he was hardly certain just *what* it was.

Had this mysterious awakening kept him from reading the intentions of this female hunter? Besides attempting to see into her mind before leaving, he had tried to go beyond the usual sedation that persuaded a victim to give their blood and then forget it had happened. Normally, he avoided linking with their thoughts and going deeper than the seduction itself required—he would merely control them and was not interested in anything beyond that.

But when he had tried to venture further with Kimberley, he could not. Why?

Had his initial bite somehow brought out an inner strength Kimberly hadn't possessed before? He had heard many tales of how a vampire could transform a victim—

both in good and bad extremes—after an encounter. However, he hadn't gone back to any one bite to witness the effects firsthand. A couple of his brothers had occasionally entertained themselves with the power of a bite on a human, taking a detached interest in how the mortals changed their lifestyles. Some became empowered, some showed latently emerged talents such as physical agility or increased charisma.

Yet not all the changes were positive.

Proof came in the form of Stephen's creator, Fegan, who often bragged about the days when he would take advantage of a victim's craving for another bite. Like Stromboli, Fegan would control his sexually awakened prey and command them to obey his every depraved whim, just like puppets on invisible strings.

As Stephen's body cut through the night air, over the mouth of the Grand Canyon, where his family had relocated approximately ten years ago, he forced himself to forget the longing, the wounded expression he had left on his latest victim and, instead, to concentrate on the reason he had left his home tonight in the first place—the rogue vampire, a creature Stephen needed to find before the criminal exposed *all* of them.

Fegan was not certain which vampire clan this rogue hailed from, but the elder vampire didn't care. Like other masters in this area, Fegan wanted the rogue quieted so they could all resume hunting the fertile grounds of nearby Las Vegas. While hiding more than usual until this rogue was caught, most vampires were taking a united stand against the criminal, and Stephen was the one charged with bringing him in.

Slowing, Stephen eased into the deeper shadows of the

canyon, his gaze honing in on the hint of a cavern's mouth while the wind chafed against him. Besides the danger this rogue vampire presented to the lifestyle of every local creature, there were other reasons Fegan had given Stephen the task of discovering the criminal's identity.

First and foremost, their leader had quite the ego, and he was angered that a fellow creature had the temerity to openly feed and, thus, put Fegan's very existence in jeopardy.

Yes, it was all about Fegan, not merely the principle. Not merely survival, either.

Before Stephen could think about the other reasons his creator had assigned him to this mission, he whisked into a buried entrance, coming to his feet in an effortless, walking landing. A soft breeze whistled around him, moaning, occasionally crying through the tunnel he followed.

Gradually, an echo of voices and laughter led him to a massive cavern, decorated with the gilded greed of a vampire gang's spoils. The baroque style included candelabras filched and transported from various European palaces, a chandelier culled from a luxury hotel in London, even a tile mural nicked from under the nose of a collector of Roman artifacts in Naples. The gang had enjoyed that particular robbery to its limits, speedily and carefully removing each tile while one of their members seduced the owner and then fed off of him.

Under the faded colors of the mural—which had originally graced the walls of an ancient brothel and depicted men and women in flagrante delicto—a group of Stephen's vampire siblings gathered. The five of them were sharing two human victims, who were still dressed in rugged outdoor clothing. Hikers. Stephen knew that the gang would only have grabbed them and brought them back if the humans had been silly enough to be wandering where canyon rules barred them from doing so. Careless.

The scent of their blood lured him, even as it pushed him away. Much about his past had repelled him for decades—all the spoils, the violence, the greed. Still, it was how he had lived, and he was not certain there was any other way to go through life, to make the nights interesting enough to tolerate.

He was what he was.

While one of his brothers—Henry D'Amato, an early gang member—raised his head and smiled at Stephen with bloodstained lips, he sensed a heavy gaze upon his back. He coolly turned around to find Fegan watching him.

The creator was sprawled in a velvet-lined chair, basking under a giant portrait of Marie Antoinette. A corpulent fellow, Fegan preferred baggy trousers shoved into high boots, an untucked silk shirt with a flaring leather coat. Gaudy gem rings sparkled from each swollen finger, and traces of dried blood lingered at the corners of his mouth. He reminded Stephen of certain depictions of Dr. Faustus that he had seen in old books, complete with a devilish, dark Vandyke beard. Fegan vaguely claimed to have been made a vampire centuries and centuries ago, while in his early fifties…and there he remained.

Stephen stopped just short of musing about the discomfiting tales of excess Fegan told with such relish. Tales that most of the family turned away from in the telling, keeping their thoughts private for the most part. However, Stephen knew what most of his brothers were thinking, now that the novelty of being a vampire had gradually worn off: *What is Fegan and why does he enjoy such appetites? And since he's our father, will we become the same sort of creature eventually?*

Shielding the direction of his thoughts, Stephen nodded to his maker. "The sun is close to rising, so I called it a night."

After checking an opulent pocket watch, Fegan raised an eyebrow. "Looks to me like you had ample time left."

Stephen let it lie. Fegan enjoying baiting him, especially since the gang had relocated this past decade. It was all too obvious that Stephen did not like Vegas or the desert, and that tickled Fegan's cruel streak. In fact, he took Stephen's displeasure as a personal affront to his taste. Consequently, it was one of many issues that had led their creator to choose Stephen for the assignment of finding the rogue. Assigning "the malcontent" to dwell in a tedious place like Vegas, where everything was so easy that it made Stephen ill, was a petty power play that emphasized Fegan's place as head of the gang.

As if any of them could forget.

Nonetheless, Stephen ignored Fegan's ego and took to his work with relish. The danger this rogue presented to his vampire kind was real, especially if there were actual hunters on the case.

Fegan dropped his pocket watch back into his coat. "So tell me, Stephen, how goes your search? I do grow tired of not being able to creep into the city, having to pick at what this canyon has to offer, instead."

"If you're referring to the rogue, I don't bring news. But I have tidings that should concern you. A hunter confronted me."

The smug expression dissipated from Fegan's face. "Hunter?"

Stephen hated the rebellious feeling of satisfaction that weighed on him. It was wrong, but it felt good anyway. "Hunters. They call themselves the Van Helsing League and, rest assured, I'll be investigating them, as well as our rogue."

At the mention of Van Helsing, Fegan laughed. "Oh, the kids these days. Van Helsing, indeed. I tell you, we study how these people talk and do our best to keep up, but they're ballsy, these humans. Especially Americans."

Stephen wasn't certain of the reason, but he bristled at his maker's mocking tone. "With the spread of technology—the Internet, media, movies—these modern times present more challenges than ever, Fegan. These hunters can do more damage to us than a batch of holy items put together, and with the rogue being so careless—"

"The rogue." Fegan became serious again. "The hunters are tracking our nasty friend, too, I take it."

Finally, some understanding. "They know he's a vampire and they're savvy to our ways."

Hunters. Uninvited, memory breathed over Stephen. Kimberly—pale blue eyes, red hair, smooth skin. Intoxicating.

He could still taste traces of the woman, her blood arousing in its primitive heat. He embraced the remnants, allowing the thoughts to consume him for a beat longer. As he relived the moment when his teeth sank into her soft neck, a rush of power surged, piercing his nerve endings, electrifying him. A shudder of ecstasy rippled down his skin and he closed his eyes.

What was he tasting? What was it about her that exposed something undiscovered within him?

Stephen opened his eyes, trying to identify this quality that he had not felt since…since he was human.

Fegan sat back in his chair, inspecting him, his expression unreadable.

Stephen straightened up, banishing tonight's bite from his mind. Why should this Kimberly be any different from other meals?

Forget her, he thought. An attachment will only end badly. You cannot bear the disappointment of losing someone—not again. Existence stretches too long for you to outlive the pain.

The sad thing was that, if he were still human, he might have given in to what he was fighting. But a vampire was made to live beyond human years, made to endure most of what might destroy him.

"I wonder," Fegan said idly, playing with his watch's gold chain, "how you know about tonight's hunter. How did he mark you as a vampire?"

"She," Stephen said, fortifying himself against more thoughts of this Kimberly. "*She* experienced my bite almost a year ago."

"And she remembers?"

Again, Stephen's skin caught erotic fire. Her skin, the scent of it, the *taste* of it… "Yes, she somehow remembered."

Fegan's fingers stilled on his watch chain. "Occasionally that happens. It did to me only… Yes, two centuries ago. Not every human has a mind of mush, so there's more work to be done with certain individuals. I expect you'll be tracking her down again and persuading her that vampires don't exist?"

Track her down again. It was all Stephen wanted to do, all his body craved in spite of his better sense.

Even so, Fegan's grand tone irked Stephen. Years—

centuries—of being ordered about had built to a shrill crescendo. "I'll do what I must, Fegan."

"Cheeky boy. If you fail us, there'll be a big price to pay."

Famous last words. Fegan had muttered them before every job, before every time the gang had struck, whether it was on a lone, wooded road outside London or a stealthy attack on an antebellum Southern home while the War Between the States had raged on in a nearby battlefield. Being ordered around had become very old.

In fact, it had gotten old with other members of their group, who had struck off on their own. None of their names were ever to be spoken in front of Fegan for fear of a temper fit.

Tauntingly, Stephen bowed to his creator. "I don't remember ever failing my family before, my *master.*"

"There's always a first time."

With all tonight's pressure, inward and out, Stephen felt ready to explode with anger. It was a mild substitute for the tension he was feeling due to… No, he was not going to think about her again; this *bite* that had suddenly taken over his world.

Needing an outlet, he took a threatening step toward his maker, and Fegan's eyes widened.

A rough female voice tinted with French put a halt to the standoff.

"To think," she said, "I was very much enjoying a snack until this interruption."

Stephen turned to find Gisele licking blood from her lips as she swayed toward them. She was the only female among the gang, a latecomer who had followed them around in Paris when they'd paid a visit in the 1970s and wheedled her way into Fegan's affections. She had been an underground cinema snob, a lonely, confused new vampire, who had been kicked out of her home when her parents grew afraid of her changed ways, and forced her to more or less live on the streets. An "adopted" child—a vampire made by another maker—Gisele had worked hard to prove she was worthy of the gang. She had learned every angle of the thievery that allowed them comfort, and she was invaluable when it came to luring victims with her feminine wiles. She was smart, self-educated, from a poor background—just as Stephen—yet more willing than any of them to embrace modern ways.

This was evident in her wardrobe. Tonight she was wearing a tight, sheer white business shirt under a form-fitting vest with a slim tie at her throat. But she also sported a very short skirt and high go-go boots; a look that complemented her razored, shoulder-length black hair. Her big, light brown eyes seemed innocent, but Stephen knew better.

"Don't you have more blood to suck, Gisele?" he asked.

"Done for the night, *Monsieur* Fangslinger," she said, passing Stephen and tweaking his long coat. Then she climbed up the few steps to where Fegan was lounging.

Sitting in his lap, she cuddled against him. He smiled, nuzzling the top of her head, content.

Their lazy, intimate posture dug at Stephen, unearthing something even deeper than what he'd felt inside earlier tonight, something terribly vague. A time in Savannah, Georgia, when a woman in a peignoir would watch for him from an upstairs window and he would come to her by moonlight. But, eventually, there'd been a night when she'd discovered what he really was, and the mask of horror that had altered her beautiful face chased any warmth out of Stephen now. She had gone on to forget him, leaving him still longing for her, still coming to her window even after her funeral. He had been as young as ever, eternally thirty-one years old, unchanged except for the newfound agony.

That was when Stephen had learned never to feel again.

To the back of him, he sensed the rest of the gang deserting their prey, leaving the humans' hearts beating while the victims languished in a blank afterglow. Later, the vampires would heal the mortals, then return them to where they had been found. At that point, the hikers' minds would be so muddled that they would not remember what had happened in the canyon.

Unlike Kimberly...

Stephen glanced behind him at his comrades, males dressed like the humans of today in jeans and casual shirts. No elegance in these times.

What had happened to all of them?

Another of the original gang, Roger, who had been born into vampirism during the mid1700s along with Stephen, winked at his friend, telling him to calm his temper and humor Fegan.

It was the easiest way to exist.

"Get some rest, Stephen," their leader said, petting Gisele's hair. "You've got a lot of work ahead of you."

The rogue. The hunters.

Kimberly.

"Yes," Stephen said, adopting a casual smile, a devil-may-care shield, "I certainly do."

And with a tight bow, he retreated to his fellow vampire brothers.

THE NEXT NIGHT fell over the city like a summer shroud, warm and veiled.

Kim was ready to go early, eager and waiting outside the Mystique nightclub long before its doors were ready to open. But she was patient, mostly because she wasn't sure she should be doing what she was doing.

She'd told the League that she would come to headquarters later tonight, that she was feeling sick and needed a little rest after working at the bookstore all day. Darlene, who would be taking her turn on League patrol with Troy inside Mystique, had offered to bring Kim chicken soup and chocolate, bless her heart.

Yet, instead of being bed-bound, Kim had armed up, not only with tools that would fight off an uncooperative vampire, but also with...well, herself.

She only hoped that would be enough to attract Stephen again.

Dressed to lure, she'd chosen a white silk top that draped over her breasts in barely concealed invitation, as well as sleek black pants and boots. She'd worn her hair back in an equally elegant ponytail, unable to resist advertising to Stephen—if he was out there—that her neck was his for the taking.

And as for last night's bite wound? She'd boldly drawn a primal design around it, disguising the quickly healing punctures while advertising them to a more knowing eye, hint hint.

On the practical side, she'd slung a little purse bulging with a vial of holy water and a crucifix over her shoulder, then traveled to Mystique. There, she'd ensconced herself in a twilight-bruised, foliage-laden cove where preopening cocktails were served. Misters tamed the warm air and caught the hard marble skin of statues positioned among the trees and bushes. A few other early birds lingered in the dark corners of the garden, too—couples who were avoiding detection.

As Kim waited, she told herself for the thousandth time that she was being stupid. Sure, she'd left a long note in her apartment explaining what she'd done—heading out alone to hopefully meet a vampire. The message was there in case she disappeared or showed up in the hospital with her blood drained, just like yet another victim last night. Thing was…

Kim frowned. This latest victim had been found in an alley on the Strip *across* from the Marrakech Casino and the Mystique nightclub. And she thought she remembered Stephen telling her that *he* wasn't the one draining these women.

But her mind was fuzzy on that. She thought she recalled asking him, then getting a reassuring answer. She just couldn't picture the details.

At any rate, after being with Stephen twice now, she hadn't been drained. And if the "bad vampire" wasn't Stephen, what if he could help her track this other creature down? Could she persuade him to answer a few questions while giving him another taste of her?

The blood seemed to swirl in her veins. She knew she wanted more out of Stephen than that. Last night's conversation with Darlene hit full force.

Make yourself un*forgettable,* her friend had said.

That's right—be somebody to him, Kim thought. Be more than just a faceless nothing who's here today and gone tomorrow.

She lifted her face to catch the light spray from a mister. Moisture settled over her skin, sucking the silk of her top to her chest. Her nipples puckered against the material, and she leaned back, feeling sensual, ready for anything.

"I'm here," she whispered, setting up to entrap her quarry. *Come and get me.*

When she felt a whoosh of air, she sat up, digging her hand into her purse. She recognized the scent that enveloped her—a mysterious essence of the unknown.

"You should have stayed home, Kimberly."

At his words, a thread of danger went taut within her, singing with a thrill. She clasped the crucifix, on alert.

Lowering her chin, she made a point of still arching her back, knowing the water had done its best to reveal everything underneath her top. Her gaze focused on Stephen, and the oxygen twisted in her lungs.

When he skimmed a gaze over her chest, every part of her tensed to pained stimulation. The sharpness ebbed to a throb, a slow melt that ended between her legs.

He was dark in this tree-covered cove she'd chosen, but the breadth of his shoulders under that outlaw coat brought back every memorized detail of him, every heart-stopping nuance.

"How could I stay away?" she asked, voice throaty. "They found another woman across the street last night, and I was hoping for a little enlightenment." She smiled and couldn't help adding, "And maybe more."

"A third bite?" He shook his head. "Didn't last night teach you anything?"

Yeah, she thought. *It taught me that I need to try harder with you.*

Just the scent of him brought it back—the woozy completion, the sense that Stephen could give her something that she'd needed so badly after her older sister had died.

Something she couldn't even begin to explain, even though she was drawn to him, all the same.

Then it struck her. Like Lori, Stephen was *dead.* Actually, he was *un*dead, which wasn't the same thing, but close enough.

She started to quiver, but it wasn't just out of the fear that she really *should* have stayed home, as he'd advised.

It was because something was wrong with her for wanting him like this, for enticing him and hoping he'd take her up on the offer.

Tremors along her belly traveled to her limbs. She sat up. "Aren't you here for another bite tonight, whether it's me or another woman?"

"You fed me well enough to last for a while." He took a step forward, all shadow now. "Why can't you forget about it like the other good prey?"

"Your other meals don't remember what happened to them?"

His silence was eloquent, and a tiny *bang!* jarred her. Last night, she'd been profoundly disappointed after he'd admitted to not remembering her. But she wasn't his usual bite. He'd just said so. She *was* different.

Yet… Was she unforgettable?

She teasingly parted her legs, opening herself to a gaze she could feel but not see.

Not until his green eyes began to glow.

Was she getting to him? Were his fangs emerging with the arousal?

Her blood began to pump, beating in her sex. She was everything that first bite had made her—confident, dominant, *somebody.* "You're here for a reason you don't want to admit, Stephen. Just say it." She smiled slowly. "You're addicted to me."

"I'm addicted to sustenance, nothing more. And it just so happens that I don't need any at the moment."

"You're gonna stand there telling me that those green eyes aren't blazing like lights on a slot machine that just hit the jackpot?"

His gaze intensified, and she primed herself. She was right. He craved her, he'd come back for more, and now was the right time to be asking him questions about vampires, to be investigating—

His gaze blinked off, as if he'd closed his eyes. From the measured cadence of his breathing, she could tell he was trying to get himself under control.

Dammit.

"I wish to know what you know," he said, so calm, so collected. "Last night didn't provide adequate answers."

She felt herself going hazy at the stroke of his voice. "I told you—we don't know much." Seriously? He just wanted to question her?

He sighed, and her mind went clear again.

"Hey," she said. "Did you just try to hypnotize me or something?"

"I tried to read you, yes."

His simple response took her aback. "Okay. Well, then, you know I'm not lying."

"I do not know what to make of you." He shook his head, started to say something, then stopped. "Why track monsters, Kimberly? Why must you do it?"

Instead of answering, she latched on to the word that had seemed the most agonizing for him to utter: *Monsters.* She'd never considered a creature this enchanting, this beautiful to be anything of the sort. Stephen was more like something fallen, someone who held knowledge and the promise of contentment with just one encounter.

"Monsters?" she asked.

"Anyone who lives my way is nothing but." His tone was uneven.

"But you—"

He stepped close. "Tell me everything you know."

Again, Kim felt bleary. Instead of fighting it, she went along with the dreamy flow, leaning her elbows on her spread thighs and glancing up at him from under her lashes.

"Stop trying to read me." *Just do what you did to me again. Let me feel how I felt before, and give me even more this time. Let me know that you're not going to forget me and that I'll leave some sort of impression before it's too late.*

In the silence, his eyes started to glow again.

Encouraged, Kim reached toward his belly, touching him there softly. She felt hard muscle under his fine shirt; those muscles jumped, responding.

"Seduce me again," she said, boldly slipping her fingers down, down, until she reached his cock. It was hard, too.

Gasping, she traced his arousal, skimming underneath to feel his balls. She made circles there, looking up again to find his eyes a glaring green now, to hear the breath sawing out of him.

"You seem very human," she whispered, giving him a slight squeeze that made him moan in clear surprise. "You're not like a monster at all."

When he leaned back his head in clear ecstasy, Kim canted forward, still sitting on the bench, then bent to him, intent on truly persuading him to make her the bite he'd never forget.

5

STEPHEN KNEW he shouldn't be giving in to her, but when Kimberly nudged against his penis, he couldn't stop himself.

She rubbed her mouth there, gently yet insistently. Needing something to grasp, he found her ponytail, wrapping its length around his hand while he held the back of her head and unthinkingly urged her on. All the while, he kept telling himself to put a halt to this. It wasn't the reason he had come to her tonight. It was not for a human to take the lead with him and reduce him to a dolt who could do nothing but surrender.

As she slid her hands under his long coat and to the backs of his thighs, Stephen eased his other palm to her neck, resting his thumb on her jugular.

Bang, bang…

Her heartbeat pounded into his flesh, joining with the rhythm of his own hunger for her blood. For her…

She had parted her lips and, even through his trousers, he could feel her drawing at his growing erection, pulling him into her mouth in ever-increasing excitement.

Stephen bent his head to watch, the darkness unable to hide her carnal play. His sight cut through what a human could never see in the night—her head bobbing as she worked at him. His ultrasharp hearing caught the sounds of her mewling in pleasure deep in her throat, caught the hum of modern wires vibrating the air and echoing the sensations of his awakening body.

He held back another moan, his elongated fangs scratching his bottom lip with the effort. Tenderly—much too tenderly—he stroked her red hair. It had been so long ago…so cursed long since he had allowed himself to be swayed by another. The last time had been under the hush of a Savannah moon, well over a century past with a woman who had screamed at his true face.

A rush of survival, of fear, made him wary. He lightly pulled back on the ponytail he had wrapped around his hand and, because of his strength, Kimberly gasped away from his cock, her chin tilted upward, her lips parted. He had not meant to be so forceful, but he couldn't have this. Couldn't carry through with certain trouble.

"You may not believe I am any sort of terrible creature," he said, his tone serrated, "but you are well on your way to bringing the monster out."

She smiled. Yes, *smiled,* and something in his chest was yanked out of its malaise. His blood throbbed through limbs that should have been dust by now, yet he felt so alive while gazing at her. Weak.

Kimberly rested a hand on his wrist, and he loosened his hold on her hair.

"You're trying really hard to make me think you're off-limits, aren't you?" she whispered.

"I suppose I shouldn't bother."

"No, Stephen." Her breath was coming hard now. She reached out, skimming her fingers against his cock. "You shouldn't bother, not when you seem to be all man to me."

Blood flooded to the afterburn of her touch, engorging him further. He strained against his trousers, the pressure agonizing.

Equally painful was the thought of becoming attached to one of them again. A woman. A human who would ultimately reject him because mortality required it. And he would never, ever, turn a human into what he was. The controlling Fegan forbade his children the act of making their *own* families; that was fine with Stephen. He had only once felt the compulsion, though he had never acted on it with Cassandra, his beautiful belle. Perhaps, if she had accepted him as he was, he would have gone against Fegan's rules and suffered the consequences of being hunted down and punished for procreating. But his Savannah lady had turned from him in horror at the truth, and Stephen had never thought of taking another human after that.

Angered by the betrayal of his body, Stephen let go of Kimberly. "I'm hardly a man. This form you see in front of you? It can imitate a man's desire. But it's only that. An imitation."

She was still looking up at him. He would have almost called her position subservient, but he knew better. This hunter woman would never be dominated unless it suited her needs.

"Imitation," she repeated. "Are you calling that hard-on a fake?"

He tried not to think about what was paining and swelling his nethers. "I am capable of this, but I cannot…"

Words failed him. So modest all of a sudden? Odd.

"You're saying we can't make babies," Kimberly said. "Is that it, Stephen?"

"Yes."

He hoped this news would be enough of a blow that it

would discourage *her* from getting attached, too. He had read that many human women coveted closeness and a future with their paramours. Having avoided this in his own mortal life, he was no expert, yet attempting to crush any growing hopes she might possess seemed wise.

Kimberly shook her head. "Not all of us are out for picket fences and a family in the suburbs."

When she tried to laugh, he knew that she wasn't persuaded by her own words. Actually, it was as though saying them out loud had made her think twice about them.

Then, as if to chase away the heavy mood, she stood from her bench, grabbing his coat lapels and resolutely leading him into a leafy, pitch-black cove of trees. Here, the sounds of the city faded; the beeping horns from the Strip were like subliminal notes of a forgotten song.

His body wound through itself, newly aroused.

"I'm not after what most women want, anyway," Kimberly said. "That shouldn't be a surprise to you."

"Don't tell me. You want another bite."

"I want…" She seemed on the verge of saying more.

In the dark, her expression glowed like candlelight to his vampire vision. There was something in her eyes he couldn't read—a hunger of her own, a craving so deep he couldn't even begin to interpret it.

Tentatively, she raised a hand from his lapel, her fingers hovering a whisper away from his face. Stephen held his breath, his blood chugging, the sound taking over his hearing.

When she touched his cheek, he flinched, knowing she was feeling the texture of him and realizing that he truly was an error of nature.

She brushed down to his jaw. "Cold. Like a statue with a layer of skin. But I feel heat underneath."

As she trailed down to his neck, he swallowed. For a beautiful moment, she stroked him, just as he had stroked her jugular earlier. In the pit of his belly, lust and need boiled.

"You look normal enough to me," she said.

It was hard to speak with his throat so scratchy. "Appearances are deceiving."

She leaned forward, nestling against his jugular. When she sniffed, he instinctively pressed his hand to the small of her back. He knew he would smell like the air itself; all a part of blending to endure.

"So good," she murmured. "You remind me of sitting in a meadow back home at sunset."

Waiting to see what she would do next, Stephen found himself splaying his fingers at the base of her spine, seeking her warmth. He loved the curve of a woman's back, loved the sensuous grace and art of it. Back when he had been a new vampire, he would have given up a night's haul to appreciate such a thing. In fact, years ago, he had done this many a time with many a willing victim when Fegan's gang had stopped a coach in the dead of night, asking the occupants to deliver their goods—which always included their blood.

As Kimberly slid open his shirt buttons, Stephen told himself that this was far enough. But he couldn't bring himself to move.

She ran her hands into the opening of his shirt, over his ribs, exploring, smoothing over to his back. Then she swept to the front again, her palms covering his stomach with a heat that pounded. When she traced upward to cover his chest, he fought another groan.

Thumbs, sweet mercy, her thumbs had found his nipples. She circled them. He peaked, a victim of her knowing search.

"You're doing okay in the response department," she whispered.

Then, just as naturally as you please, she bent and fixed her mouth to a nipple, tasting it with a delightfully soft touch. He dug his other hand into her hair, his base urges forcing him to slide the palm at the small of her back downward, into her clingy yet stretchy pants. She wasn't wearing undergarments, so his caress was unimpeded by lace. It was all pure skin, flushed and smooth.

Electrified, he skimmed the cleft of her rear end, then coaxed his fingers down farther to cup the curve of a cheek. He heard her zipper strain, then break.

Not that she seemed to care. With his ministrations, she winced against his chest, opening her mouth and tonguing his nipple, biting it lightly. Then, on a sudden breath, she rose, grabbed his hips and brought his erection against her belly, nestling her mouth against his neck.

With her pants much looser now, he dipped his hand lower, under her cheeks and between her legs, where he found her sex slick and hot. He strummed her there as she opened farther. She gnawed at him, making pleased little sounds.

All thoughts of the rogue vampire and the hunting group vanished like ghosts in a mist, leaving only an outline of reluctance in Stephen.

Stop, he kept thinking. *Time to stop.*

She grasped the hand he had mired in her disheveled hair, kissed his wrist, his palm, then guided his fingers to her lips.

"More man than…anyone else," she panted, taking a digit into her mouth.

She began to imitate what he was doing to her sex with his other fingers, which circled and pressed against her clitoris. Forced to his limits by her tongue, he pushed two fingers into her, and she softly cried out. Swollen, so wet.

As she continued sucking at him, he slid out, in, spreading her juices. She picked up the erotic tempo, drawing his fingers in, then out of her mouth.

Warm and wet there, too, he thought.

She sucked at him, slowly, wantonly, until there was so much tension built up in him that he thought he would burst to ragged bits.

In response, he thrust his fingers into her again, but this time he did not mark his own strength. He had lifted her so high and against him with the drive of his desire that she was draped over his shoulder, his fingers so deep into her that she groaned in both pleasure and surprise.

Horrified that he had hurt her, he let up. But when she squirmed against him, asking for more, he was shocked to discover that he wanted to give it to her.

Almost bonelessly, she slid down his body, like water over skin. Her sex stroked down his chest. Then her breasts. Then her mouth. As he held her against him, she traced her tongue over his flesh. A message, a single word.

More.

All his trepidation came flooding back, wiping him out, washing away this spell she had put him under and revealing his survival instincts.

He extracted his fingers from her. They were drenched. He shuffled away the craving to lift them to his lips, to taste her, then to sink his fangs into her for the ultimate treat. Her blood.

Two bites were excusable. But, three?

Three indicated a habit he couldn't afford.

Knowing what he had to do, he lifted Kimberly's chin until her gaze met his. Passion glowed in her pale blue eyes, almost dragging him back in. But his will wouldn't allow it.

No, even while his body screamed for her, he used his power to drive her away.

I really am a monster, he thought, using his ability to saturate a human mind. *I'll show you as much.*

With that, he slammed images designed to scare her into her head—the first time he had fed as a new vampire. The blood, the terror of not knowing what he had become. The dead body beneath him, the eyes staring dully over his shoulder at Fegan, who was laughing like a king at a banquet table. Stephen had been the third member recruited for the master's most recent gang; he'd only been a man who had taken to the roads to earn meals, a failed blacksmith who knew nothing of life except that it was hard work. But at this first feeding, none of that had mattered.

Now, after planting those images, Stephen saw the fear in Kimberly's gaze, saw that he had gotten through to her. But…

But, after the first moment, a look of sublime enlightenment captured her features. A comprehension, as if he had answered one of the many questions humans inevitably had about their existence. She hazily reached up to touch his lips, to run a finger over a fang, and he reared away.

"You are foolish," he uttered.

She grabbed his coat with more strength than he had given her credit for, hauling him back to her.

"I'm *ready*," she said.

What was she seeing in him besides the ugly truth? What would it take to knock some sense into her?

Into *him?*

"Shh," she said, calming him while drawing him farther into the cove. "I can handle anything, Stephen. Try me."

Now he knew that he had chosen to be with a woman who was daft. But he didn't truly believe that. There was something else happening inside of her and, much to his chagrin, it intrigued him. Compelled him.

"Shh," she repeated while caressing his neck, "I want you to remember this, remember everything about this night."

"That's a certainty." He was throbbing again.

With another bold smile, she gently pulled his head down to meet her. She kissed him, her mouth barely brushing his. Her next words tickled his lips.

"Unlike a regular man, you're showing fangs."

He drew back, knowing this wasn't a good thing. But she wouldn't let him go.

"I like that, Stephen. I've fantasized about that for the past year."

"It's not a healthy fetish."

"Says who?" She lifted her mouth to his again. "Now be quiet while I take care of some wish fulfillment."

Thrown off balance—never in his existence had he met a woman so determined and impervious—Stephen could do nothing but comply. What was he saying? He *wanted* to comply; it was not as if he were a bite-addled servant.

Before Kimberly's lips met his, she lightly outlined his mouth with her finger. He shivered. When she reached the bottom, she took his lips between her index finger and thumb and—

He heaved in a breath at the sting.

She had pinched his lips together, and the pleasant pain jolted him, excited him. Before he could recover, she tugged him nearer, sucking his lower lip into her mouth, then capturing all of him.

His hands hovered in the air, helpless as she seduced him with a leisurely kiss. She dove in deep with her tongue, exploring him, flirting with his fangs in confident wickedness. She had to know that, when aroused by the possibility of feeding, his teeth extended in preparation, much like other uncontrollable parts of his body.

Parts that were pounding out demands even now.

Slowly, he gave in, ensnared by stirred sensations he had kept long hidden.

At her kiss, images of him as a mortal, as a servant on his master's country estate, flowed through him. Peace, he thought, remembering the muted gurgle of a stream as it meandered through a field. As a vampire, that gurgle would have sounded like a gush; even soft murmurings had the power to overwhelm until Fegan had taught him how to shut out the noise, to restrain and subdue.

But now, Stephen felt no restraint, and that was foreign to a creature who had learned to turn off the infusions life assaulted him with nightly.

As Kimberly sipped at his lips, he found himself pulling her against him. Each of her curves melded into him, fused by his cravings, each wild heartbeat in her body becoming his own.

Then, with even more passion—how she managed to conjure more, he did not know—she devoured him. He returned each nip, each suck, until he felt weak all over. Warm, altered, melted.

"More," she whispered harshly, pushing the hair that had come out of her ponytail away from her neck. "More, Stephen."

No. He wouldn't bite her again.

Then, obviously knowing him too well, even in such a short time, she made a sound that resembled a frustrated growl, going for his throat and…

Stephen reared his head back, stunned. She was sucking at his neck like a starved animal. His body seemed filled with gunpowder, shooting, stinging beneath his skin. Destructive flashes pounded at him with their spark, destroying him from the inside out. And it was not merely a physical decimation—the explosions chipped away at his unwillingness to ever get close to one of them again. Each pop and bang exposed him, leaving him vulnerable.

Summoning all his rage—all the self-loathing he had cultivated—Stephen extricated himself from her. Yet, even as he did it, the forced distance felt wrong, unnatural.

In a last-ditch effort to preserve himself, he bared his fangs, knowing he looked like the monster he actually was. He knew his eyes held eviscerating fire, his mouth held the promise of a screaming death.

As Kimberly backed away, her eyes widening at what he had changed into, something heavy fell from his chest to his stomach.

"Is this your fantasy?" he growled. "Am I all you and your hunters had ever hoped for, Kimberly?"

She opened her mouth to speak, but nothing emerged.

Then, just to be certain this would never happen again, he added, "I am death. Do you understand? I am not a man at all."

And, before he could change his mind, he flew away from her once more, a creature who had become a part of the night he belonged to.

MEANWHILE, nearby, the rogue vampire made yet another desperate attempt to get someone to notice him. Anyone. Because eventually this would lead to his dearest wish—becoming one of *them* again. A mortal. A being who had no idea how beautiful a limited life was.

He lingered at the Marrakech casino's bar tonight. Long ago, a host had invited him into the building as he'd strolled by on the sidewalk, therefore accidentally choosing where the rogue would drain the first victim, then most of the others. Here, neon blended, making everything an eye-stinging blur.

This time he had done his research, preselecting a victim who would definitely force some recognition. He would make sure his message would be about more than merely a draining. If tonight's bite didn't draw out his ultimate prey—or even a representative of him—the rogue didn't know what would.

As a part of that research, he had read the papers, then turned to the Internet to see what other avenues he could discover for subtle publicity—the kind that would only threaten exposure to the humans, not guarantee it.

Now his endgame could be won. At least, he hoped so. Even though he had led a long existence, he'd become so tired lately. The last of his will was drained, and he was ready. He was eager for everything to finally change.

When he saw tonight's victim and her friend meander past the gaming tables on the way to the Mystique nightclub, he tossed a few dollars onto one of the video poker screens that littered the bar, the bills coming to rest against his untouched gin and tonic. Then he trailed his prey, gaze assaulted by the blinking slot machines until he concentrated on tuning it all out.

She got in a long line snaking past a gift shop and

waited along with the other hopefuls, all so young and fresh in their slinky clothes and overactive hormones. As a group of girls glanced at him and smiled, he tried to be pleasant while not encouraging them. It worked.

Soon, the club opened, the line moving enough for him to enter only three parties behind his chosen victim. He focused on her, catching a whiff of her scent through the stale cigarette smoke. Her hair, worn up in a bun, revealed her lovely neck. Once inside, he waited, ensconcing himself in the stereo-pulsing shadows while everyone else danced and drank and forgot to remember to count the blessings that every second of mortality afforded them.

They all should be living every moment as if it were their last. Only a vampire knew how precious that was, because urgency lost its meaning over too many years. It lost its value.

Though his intended victim was with a man, there came a time when one went to the restroom while the other hung back. It just so happened that it was his prey who needed to visit the facilities first. Like a streak of Vegas light, the rogue vampire followed her inside and slipped into her private stall before she—or anyone else—could detect him.

But they wouldn't be here for long; he planned to subdue her, then use his preternatural speed to spirit her off to a more private location. The rogue would wait and hope for any enforcers there, wait and hope for as long as it took.

As she saw him suddenly standing in front of her, she screeched in a breath. He mildly put his hand over her mouth before she could make a sound.

Then he divested her of her bulging shoulder bag before she could move to stop him.

There was a line of women outside giggling as they waited for their turn in a stall. They had no idea.

The rogue looked into his woman's eyes, captivating her. *There's no reason to scream.*

Gradually, her eyes went from wide to glossy. He removed his hand from her mouth. Her lips remained moist, parted, her scent blood-laced and fearful. His fangs emerged in anticipation of what this bite would finally bring him. *Mercifully* bring him.

Quiet now, he told her silently. *I'm going to make you feel very good, dear.*

And he proceeded to do just that, his shadow covering her in darkness as he leaned forward to drink.

6

As Kim rode the elevator to her apartment, she tried to think about what had happened back at Mystique. But her brain wasn't working right, and it wasn't just muddled from what she thought might be a touch of hypnosis from Stephen, either. It was filled with a jittery terror.

An addictive wariness.

Even though she was shaken, she was stirred up. Stephen's true vampire form had done its job in frightening her off at first, but... Dammit, she had to admit it— the sight of him so dangerous, so hungry had only brought her to the next level of... What? Obsession?

Was she some kind of junkie with latent adrenaline cravings? Was she an insatiable superfreak vampire groupie?

What was with her?

The elevator dinged and opened the doors to her floor. The lobby was a modest mix of Spanish tile and iron-laced wall decorations, a middle-rent haven. She walked past all of it in a daze.

Once again, the image of Stephen turning fully, furiously into a vampire assaulted her. Fangs extended all the way until they were like saber teeth, eyes blazing with what she could only describe as ferocious...

She stopped walking, leaning against the wall, resting

her hand on it for balance as she closed her eyes. Her pulse picked up steam, her nerve endings on fire.

I am death, he'd said. *Do you understand?*

A horrible thought cut through everything else. Death. Did Stephen represent what was waiting for them all?

His altered appearance remained rooted to the backs of her eyelids, so Kim opened her gaze, clinging to what she *wanted* to see in Stephen—her fantasy, her sexual ideal.

Well, she was a real piece of work. In lust with something that scared her, intrigued her, called to her. She'd pleased him tonight, even without a bite, and that somehow satiated her. Having made him so helpless told her she was everything she'd hoped to become after that first bite—in control, desirable, memorable. She'd had him at her mercy—she knew it—and he was certainly never going to forget her.

But was that enough?

No, she thought. She wanted him to need her again and again, in spite of everything. She wanted an actual feeding, not just foreplay.

At the sound of a door opening, she composed herself, pushing away from the wall and yanking her coat over the slinky silk blouse. In her car, she'd fixed her hair back into its ponytail—the one Stephen had ruined, when she'd gone full throttle for her fantasies.

Kim found herself smiling, ridiculing herself. She'd given Stephen a hickey. *A hickey.* How many of his bites did that to him?

When she rounded the corner into the hallway, she found Mr. and Mrs. Cornish gussied up for a night on the town—if that was what you would call the suburban Green Valley area of Henderson. The couple, who were on the sunset side of their seventies, were "foodies" and, besides attending every cocktail show in town, they made a frequent practice of going to new, trendy restaurants whenever they could get reservations. It was a bonus that Kim could always catch the aroma of amazing meals from her neighbors' apartment, too.

"Late grub tonight?" Kim asked, hoping she didn't look as spooky as she'd been feeling. That'd be mortifying.

Mr. Cornish beamed at her. Both he and the missus were short, with impishly twinkling blue eyes, but Sean Cornish had spiky gray hair to Caroline's meticulous bob.

"We've already indulged in a phenomenal meal," he said in his Bah-ston accent.

Mrs. Cornish joined in, her rosy cheeks just as effusive as her personality. "Yes, I made a lovely Grilled Berkshire Pork Chop. I'll call you over next time we have it. But we're off to see the cocktail show at New York, New York, now, you know. They've got a *disco* band in the Big Apple Lounge."

While his wife talked, Kim felt Mr. Cornish's scrutiny, wondering just what the ex-cop was thinking. She drew her coat tighter around her body, smiling and nodding as Mrs. Cornish finished her commentary.

"You in for the night already?" he asked Kim.

The Cornishes were protective of her. Their grown kids were halfway across the country, having stayed on the East Coast instead of following their retired parents to Sin City. Kim was their little project, so she did her best to hide her bad-girl activities.

"I'm in," she said, thinking that she had a lot of League work to do. She wasn't going to be getting any information about the drainer vampire from Stephen tonight. More importantly, he was probably done with her—at least, for the time being. But if she'd succeeded in any way, he'd be back.

Hopefully.

"No shenanigans for this young blood," Mr. Cornish said. "Miss Kim's usually out later."

"Just tired." A convenient yawn came upon Kim. "I'm not a party animal like you all."

"I hope you're not catching anything." Mrs. Cornish wrinkled her brow. "They say there's something going around."

Is there ever, Kim thought.

Mr. Cornish tweaked his wife's pink cheek. "Leave her to her business, Caroline." Then he winked at Kim. "Don't wait up for us."

"Oh, I won't. Tonight, I don't have the energy to light up the town until the break of dawn."

As Kim raised her hand in a goodbye, she couldn't help noticing how Mr. Cornish turned back to his wife. They smiled at each other, fools in love. It caught Kim, keeping her from leaving.

Smitten for more than fifty years, she thought as the elderly couple held hands and rounded the corner toward the elevators. Kim couldn't imagine ever finding that.

She unlocked her door and, even though she tried to empty her mind, what she'd said to Stephen earlier niggled.

"Not all of us are out for picket fences and a family in the suburbs," she'd said, and she'd meant it, too. Kim wasn't the type to end up like the Cornishes. After the first bite, the life of a free bird had really appealed to her. It seemed to go well with a sexual awakening.

Right? Wasn't she happy with how she was living now?

She thought of why Lori had called her to that coffee shop where she'd died. Thought of the discussion they were going to have about the unexpected pregnancy that single-girl, Lori, had been debating about ending.

Thought of how she, prebite Kim, had been desperately trying to talk Lori into keeping the baby.

Pushing all of it away, Kim entered her abode and tossed her bag and coat on the kitchen table. Besides everything else, she had a column to write. Even though she wasn't going to record this latest encounter with Stephen, she needed to update her readers about last night's draining victim.

In her bedroom, Kim changed into something more comfortable—a cotton nightgown with flowers that reminded her of her parents' massive front yard on the outskirts of Nashville. Then she opened the window to let in the warm night air, settling in front of her laptop, which was situated at a frail desk. There, among her framed *Witchblade* comic posters and a black futon that had seen better days, she got busy, first calling Troy's cell for an update from Mystique. When he didn't answer, she tried Darlene. Same deal. Figuring they probably couldn't hear their phones over the obnoxious club music, Kim turned her attention to her column. She'd give her League partners another go soon.

She didn't know how much time had gone by; being on the computer had a way of squeezing the hours into minutes. But when she heard her name whispered, like an echo in her ears, she started in her chair, her eyes flying to a clock that told her it was past midnight.

"Kimberly," the voice said again.

Her body recognized the low timbre of it, the seductive

accent. Skin prickling, she turned toward her window, hands gripping the edge of her desk.

She found him there, waiting patiently, bobbing while floating on black air. Her heart lurched at the sight of his handsome face, which was lit only by the dim light from her apartment.

His *regular* face, thank God, not the nightmare he'd adopted just before flying away earlier.

"Stephen?" She didn't know what else to say.

Her gaze traveled to his neck, where the pink kiss of her hickey glowed against pale flesh. It was already healing.

In spite of herself, her belly clenched with desire.

For a moment, he seemed enraptured by her, but then his jaw tightened.

The memory of his terrible vampire face kept her from inviting him inside, even though she was dying to do it.

He continued floating. "While we were…occupied outside Mystique tonight, another victim was attacked inside the club."

"Another? Oh, crap."

"I could have found the culprit, if…"

He trailed off, and Kim knew exactly why. She was feeling the same way, too. If they hadn't been so engaged outside Mystique, another draining might not have happened. Stephen might have been there to interfere.

It occurred to her that maybe this was the reason Troy and Darlene weren't answering their phones. Were they hot on the trial of the draining vampire? Or…

Kim swallowed. Was the culprit maybe even right outside her window, waiting to be invited inside? Yes, Stephen had denied being the drainer, but he could be lying. He could've gone into Mystique after he'd left her so abruptly.

She gathered her guts and made like a good investigator. "I have to wonder about your proximity to this newest event."

A tight smile didn't offer any reassurance. "You're asking, once again, if I am the rogue?"

"Yup, I'm asking."

He seemed disappointed that she'd inquired, seemed relieved that she *didn't* trust him. Dammit, it was too hard to understand him.

"I'm hunting down this rogue," he said, "just as you are hunting me and my kind. My family has tasked me with stopping this mad vampire before he does irrevocable damage beyond what he inflicts on his victims."

"You're..." She stood awkwardly, her knees jellied. "You're a slayer?"

"No, I'm a vampire who must censure one who has gone against his own breed. I'm the one chosen by his master to see that we remain safely hidden."

She wanted to believe him, she really did. But was that smart?

Yeah, Kim thought. Brilliant question *now*.

"Kimberly," he whispered.

His tone had changed into that dreamy film of seduction she couldn't fight off. *Wouldn't* fight off.

Stephen held his hand to the window frame. "Let me in and we'll put an end to these attacks. We were interrupted from doing so earlier when I came to you."

And he had obviously reconsidered and tracked her down for another attempt at doing his own job.

Her common sense made one last play to resist, but her body was already halfway toward the window. "How do you plan to put an end to all this?"

He laughed, deep and trustworthy. Sexier than anything she could ever dream up.

"You'll tell me everything about what you know from your League, and I'll continue from there. Our rogue leaves no scent, no trail for me to follow from Mystique. Unlike you, none of the victims recall anything about their attacks—at least, according to news reports, since I haven't the luxury of approaching them. There are no leads beyond your League."

Compelled, willing, she opened the window all the way, and he eased inside, coming to a negligent stance on her carpet.

"No one saw you out there?" she asked, her mind beginning to clear.

"I tracked any traces of humanity, and sensed no one about."

When he stood next to her, his nostrils flared, his eyes going that sharp green she could translate now. He was turned on, maybe even yearning for a new high that only she could give him. At least, she wished.

Then, as if chastising himself, he stepped away, creating distance. The friction of their tension left only a memory of heat between them, and she felt robbed of it.

He wandered to her computer, frowned, then touched the CPU. The screen went blank, sending her column bye-bye.

Kim bolted forward. "Hey!"

"I would appreciate your discretion in our dealings, Kimberly."

"Man, if you erased my hard drive, I might be angry enough to stake you." Or to give him another hickey.

"What you know about this case—and me, in particular—must never be revealed."

"I wasn't writing about…*you.*" Weird. She was blushing. When had she developed that talent?

A strange look branded his expression, too. Part bewilderment, part…she wasn't sure, but she thought it might be tenderness.

The possibility shocked her. Scared her. It wasn't a component of the fantasy. Just completion, orgasmic oblivion. She didn't need anything besides that.

"Kimberly," he said softly, "if vampires are discovered by society at large, it would mean the end to our freedom. We would run under the threat of persecution, I've told you this before. Is this what you want for us? For…"

He turned back to the computer as if to shut himself up, but she easily completed his sentence.

For him. Is that what she wanted for *him?*

Before now, she hadn't really considered that. Stephen wasn't…quite real. Even though she'd insisted he was all man, he wasn't truly human to her. He was a dream to pursue, a goal.

But now… Now she realized he was a sentient creature who had to survive like anyone else. And her amateur hunting act had the power to hurt him.

It was like realizing Dungeons & Dragons was reality— that you could control a whole world with a game board. The League's activities could have more impact than she'd ever thought possible.

"Are you asking me to stop investigating after I've told you all I know?" she asked.

He looked up from the computer, the answer naked on his face. Yes, he was asking.

Across the room, a picture sat in a place of honor on the counter. Lori, her short red hair tousled from a day in the sun, her smile infectious. Her big sister. Her idol while she was growing up.

"You don't know *what* you're asking." Kim couldn't tear her gaze away from the image, the tragedy. "There're things I need to know, Stephen. Things I can't find in fiction or movies or rumors. I don't 'hunt' for the League. I do it for myself."

But why? she thought. Why the hell was she turning to him?

He watched her intently, but she didn't feel the dizziness that usually accompanied a vampire's attempt at hypnosis. Then, his gaze softened, as if in sympathy.

"What could I possibly tell you, Kimberly? I have no answers. None of us do."

His words were like pointed thrusts into her heart, and she sank to the floor, following the drag of her disappointment.

She hadn't known until this second how much she'd depended on getting answers from him—answers about what was waiting for all of them after the sun fell over their bodies, answers about whether there was any hope for them in the end.

As she lowered her head, she lost sight of Lori's picture.

Lost sight of everything except Stephen.

AT KIMBERLY'S disheartening reaction, Stephen darted forward, though he didn't know what he would do.

Her hitched breath revealed her own surprise at his impulsive reaction.

As he composed himself, he thought about what he had just sensed about this woman—a hint of what lay behind her need to hunt. Somehow, he knew it had nothing to do with destroying vampires—not intentionally, at least.

The mystery of her grew deeper, pulling at the ever-thickening tie that brought him back to her again and again.

Earlier, after leaving Kimberly outside Mystique in the garden area, Stephen had gone to the nightclub only to find nothing. That is, until reports of a woman lying in a construction site near the Strip filtered into his consciousness.

Heedlessly, driven by anger at the rogue as well as himself, Stephen had flown there to track his enemy, but had held off because of the police activity. With alert humans near, it would have been nigh impossible for him to perform his own detecting.

He had to keep his wits about him if he wished to succeed in this task. And he *had* to succeed, or else all vampires might pay for his failure. He had to react with cool, measured logic from this point on, not hot-blooded instinct.

Fegan wouldn't be happy at all. Then again, Stephen didn't give a toss. He wasn't doing this for the approval of his master. He didn't require it.

As Kimberly gritted her jaw and wiped the tears from her face—as in control as he expected her to be—Stephen distanced himself. Her emotion moved him and he couldn't countenance that. Still, he fought the urge to touch her, to comfort her. The fact that she was wearing an innocent nightgown sprigged with flowers nearly undid him, as well. The paradox of the woman who had naughtily seduced him earlier and the softer version of this Kimberly moved him.

How could he have forgotten that first bite with her?

He knew. She had gained confidence from their initial encounter, and that was why he couldn't bring himself to stay away from her now. She was strong, bold, soft. Fascinating.

"Shoot," she said from her sitting position, clearly hating the tears, "crying isn't doing any good."

He wanted to tell her that tears were a gift, that caring enough to weep should be treasured. To a vampire such as him, it was rare to be affected enough to show emotion.

When she looked up at him with those sad eyes, he almost lost hold of himself. Something inside of him jerked and twisted with light before the darkness snuffed it out again.

Her phone rang, and he turned his back on her, unable to bear one more moment. He heard her scramble up from the floor, then fumble with the communication device.

He couldn't quite decipher the bit his hearing could catch.

"Hello? Troy? Jeez, I tried to call you earlier but... Emergency? I can't... This is a bad connection. What?" She was quiet for a few seconds. Then, the words gushed out of her. "Where are you? Is she doing okay? Oh, God... Troy? Tr—"

She slammed the phone down and he turned to find her dashing toward a bedroom, her nightdress billowing out behind her.

He followed, lingering in the doorway.

She was jerking a tank top out of a drawer, her face a riot of devastation at whatever news she had just heard. Without paying attention to him, she tugged off her nightgown, revealing her body in all its glory. He told himself to look away.

But...no. He wasn't able to.

Those full breasts, that flat stomach, the long legs. The pale, smooth skin...

His fangs emerged, pulsing in time to his cock. Stephen fought himself, averting his eyes, but that didn't erase the fragrance of her skin, the blood thudding just below the surface of her flesh.

"I've got to go," Kimberly said.

"I have a feeling this concerns vampires." He cleared his throat of its debris. "If not, I can help with any…"

She had stopped dressing, and he chanced a look at her. She was garbed in a gray tank top and faded jeans. One boot was on and the other off, the shoe hanging in her hand as she measured him with a haunted gaze.

"Any private matters," he finished, mouth dry.

She kept staring at him, and he could not help thinking that she was debating the wisdom of sharing the call's contents. Finally, she continued putting on her boot, stomping into it.

"You're going to find out, anyway." Stomp. "One of the League…my friend…Darlene, she…" Kimberly stomped again, but her boot was already on. She stood, hands on hips, calming herself. "Darlene was the victim in Mystique tonight. They've got her at the E.R."

Without hesitation, Stephen left the doorway.

"Wait!" Kimberly yelled, catching up to him and taking hold of his coat.

"You stay here. I'll find a way to talk to this Darlene, to look into her mind and try to discover what she saw."

Kimberly laughed, and it wasn't because he had been joking. It was one of those sarcastic laughs some humans excelled at.

"You don't appreciate my orders," he guessed.

"No, I don't. I'm either flying the friendly skies with you or driving to Darlene myself. My gut is telling me to hop in the car *without* you, because I don't know what to make of all this, Stephen. You could be more dangerous than anything…if you're not this rogue vampire himself."

"Oh, yes." Sarcasm came out in his tone now. "I've taken the trouble of coming here to you, exposing myself, and I now I wish to show my face to this Darlene so she may identify me. I'm a criminal genius."

She paused, then shrugged. "Just being a careful girl."

"It would be for the first time, don't you think?"

A red tinge colored her skin, and Stephen blinked, just to see if he was mistaken. Yes, she was blushing. He hadn't expected the reaction to be in her nightly repertoire.

She seemed to notice it, as well. As she darted ahead of him, she said, "Let's get a move on."

It was what they called "a brush-off."

"I wish you would stay out of this," he said wearily.

"Your wish isn't my command. Boy, I know you're probably a really ancient vampire and everything, but an oldfangled He-Man attitude doesn't go far with me." She grabbed her bag from the kitchen table and headed for the door. "You're not going to keep me out of this."

He almost told her that he didn't want to see her hurt, but the words were too difficult to utter. They would have meant he was feeling protective.

When she bolted through the doorway and didn't find him behind her, she turned on him. "What? This rogue just got to my friend. *My friend.* He attacked her, and that pisses me off. Is it so bad to be looking for a bit of justice?"

It hit him full in the chest—he couldn't control her. Even if he were to stun her with his mind, he had the feeling Kimberly wouldn't take to it. This was a woman who recalled details of his first bite, so chances seemed dim for relying on her cooperation.

If she insisted on continuing, he could wage his own

battle and control her in his own way. By joining her in an investigation tonight, he could be privy to the same information; he could monitor what she intended to put on her League's Internet site.

Working with her was making more and more sense.

Stephen nodded, and she didn't even wait for him to reach the door before sprinting away. All he wanted to do was chase her down, make sure she didn't get herself hurt, but he stopped himself.

The attachment would have to be snipped off before it became stronger than he could handle.

7

"It's just all a blur," Darlene mumbled from her hospital bed as Kim gently clutched her friend's hand.

Darlene's normally olive-toned skin was pale, rivaling the bed sheets. Her dark curly hair was springing out of its bun, a reflection of the chaos she'd survived. Luckily, some drunken tourists had found her at the edge of the construction site, where the rogue vampire had evidently left her to be discovered.

Why had he or she done that? Kim didn't know. But the vamp's change in M.O. was strange enough to have inspired her and Stephen to toss around theories on the way over.

Now Kim maintained her grip on Darlene's hand, questions about the rogue all but forgotten. With IV tubes decorating her friend's arm, Kim wasn't focusing properly. Instead, she held on even tighter, just as she would've done to her sister, Lori, if she'd had the chance.

The hospital room's antiseptic stench made Kim push back a wave of nausea. "It's understandable that things are cloudy, Dar. You don't have to remember it all right now. Just rest. There'll be plenty of time later."

She heard the rest of the League—Troy, Jeremy and Powder—shuffling their feet behind her. Who could blame them for being impatient about finding out what'd happened to one of their own?

Then she glanced at the stranger among them—Stephen.

She'd told her friends that her vampire was a "date" who had refused to desert her in a time of need, and Stephen had adjusted his appearance to support the charade. He'd undone his dark blond hair so that it brushed his shoulders, plus shed his long coat to reveal a natty white shirt and trousers. He was doing a good job of passing as her human companion, but that wasn't surprising. In any given situation, Stephen *had* to fit in.

And he really did seem so normal, standing in the corner, silently taking in every one of Darlene's soft words.

But Kim knew he was far from it, even if he was a master of simple disguise. When he'd stopped short of the hospital's threshold earlier, she realized that he probably needed to be invited in, so she'd done the honors.

Still, he really did look so human.

A dark hunger rushed through her. It was the only thing making her feel right now, the only thing keeping her from losing composure as she compared Darlene to Lori, who hadn't been lucky enough to survive something far more normal. If you could call a car crashing into the front window of a diner "normal."

Tears rushed Kim, and she clasped her other hand over Darlene's. Thank God Dar was still here. Thank God.

Her friend smiled weakly in reassurance, seeming to recognize what Kim was undergoing.

"Hey, girl," she said.

Kim leaned forward.

"I'm gonna be fine." Darlene closed her brown eyes,

then slowly opened them, clearly still feeling the effects of her medication.

Kim held on tighter, hoping there'd be no trauma for her friend, only a good sleep.

"Maybe we should leave her alone," Jeremy whispered.

He was right, but Kim had a hard time dragging herself away. She kissed Darlene on the forehead, taking a moment to brush some hair away from her friend's cheek, then let Powder assume his place by the bed to keep watch.

He held a crucifix in one hand and dropped a gym bag on the floor near his scrawny ankle. Kim could discern the outline of a wooden stake pressing against the nylon. Weapons.

Then Stephen wandered over to the now-resting Darlene, and Kim wondered what the hell he was doing. But when he touched her friend's bite, then her temple, she knew.

She caught the rest of the League while they walked out the door and cast curious glances at Stephen.

"He's never seen a bite before," she said, shrugging and hoping that would do for an excuse.

When Stephen was done trying to heal Darlene and read her thoughts, Kim took one last look at her friend, who was smiling in her sleep now, probably because of the vamp's touch. The bunch of them left, passing a few cops lingering outside the door in the aftermath of their questioning. They were stymied by this latest case of severe blood loss, and part of Kim wished that they would just open their eyes and accept the obvious truth. The other part of her wanted them to stay ignorant, and she knew it was only because Stephen would benefit from that.

As Kim sorted out the contradictions, she and her

friends gravitated to the lobby, which blinked under a dead-of-night fluorescent glow.

Near the reception desk, a few doctors wandered over the white tiles, checking charts, shooting glances at the League every so often. Kim turned away from them to face Troy and Jeremy, who ignored the waiting seats and remained standing.

Stephen lingered on the edges of their group, a presence that obviously rankled the boys, especially Troy.

Their leader was keeping an eye on "Kim's date." Hell, he was doing a pretty great job of checking out the fake tattoo she'd scrawled on her neck to hide last night's bite, too. Nosy guy. Thank God she'd been too eager to work on her column to scrub the design off earlier. Troy would've called her on the bite for certain.

"I told you," Kim said, ignoring her coworker's scrutiny. "You can talk in front of Stephen. He reads the Web site and listens to our broadcasts all the time."

Troy still didn't look convinced, but why should she expect him to be? Earlier, he'd been the only one to protest Stephen being in Darlene's hospital room.

However, Kim had won that little standoff when Darlene had woken up and started talking. Then, everyone had forgotten everything but their friend, though Stephen was definitely still on Troy's watch list.

Their leader jammed a hand through his blond hair and positioned himself to halfway face Stephen, who was leaning against a pole, his expression neutral under the other guy's bristling attention.

She cleared her throat, drawing the group leader's gaze. "So did *you* see anything tonight, Troy? Weren't you Darlene's wingman during patrol?"

"Yeah, I was."

Troy looked disgusted with himself, and Jeremy awkwardly patted him on the back, red creeping over the sensitive senior's cheeks as he adjusted his black-framed glasses.

"But," Troy added, "she had to go to the bathroom at some point. I watched her walk through the door and never saw anyone suspicious follow her inside. Except…"

"What?" both she and Jeremy asked.

Troy's forehead furrowed. "Except, I thought I *felt* something. Maybe. A breeze rushed past before the door closed, and then a few minutes later, but…man, what if that was the vamp going after her and taking her away?"

Jeremy shifted, his eyes widening under the glasses. He didn't look very comfortable.

Kim glanced at Stephen, who was reacting like any other League site reader would've reacted—an interested party who didn't want to interrupt. He gave nothing else away.

"I have a theory," Kim said, recalling how Stephen had a thing for taking off in flight. "This vampire can move faster than our eyes can detect. Maybe he swept Dar right out of that bathroom while only slowing down a hair on the way out because of her added weight."

From the slight cock of Stephen's brow—an approving gesture—she knew she was close, if not absolutely right. This was no time for tingles, but she got them anyway. How could she help it around him?

Troy crossed his arms over his wide chest. "All I know is that I kept looking at my watch and she kept not coming out. Darlene isn't the type to primp for too long, so I asked another woman to look for her inside."

Kim was sure that her handsome coworker hadn't experienced too much trouble in persuading a gal to help him out.

She snagged Stephen's considering glance as it grazed over her, then Troy. She frowned, sending the signal that nothing was going on between the two of them.

Dummy. Didn't he know it was all about him? If he didn't realize that, she still had some major work to do.

She thought of how hard she'd fought to have him bite her earlier and how he'd refrained from doing so. Her chest contracted as she tried to tell herself that she could still win him over. *Had* to, because getting bitten had come to mean so much more than just being an object of his desire.

She brushed aside the distraction. Darlene was lying on a hospital bed. There had to be answers—maybe even more than Stephen's bite might give her.

"And that other woman who went inside the bathroom," Kim said to Troy, more determined than ever. "She didn't find anything?"

"Just a locked and empty stall." Troy shook his head. "She and her friends peeked into all of them, even waited for other women to come out of the occupied ones… Darlene didn't have any blood on her when she was found, so she didn't even leave a trail. There was nothing. And, when the cops got there, they didn't find a damned clue, either."

At the word *damned,* Stephen stirred, brow furrowed in apparent unease. It was all Kim could do to keep herself from going to him, touching him, making him as relaxed as he'd been earlier when they'd had their encounter outside of Mystique.

Jeremy piped up, "So the cops didn't find a thing until they got the call about Darlene propped up against a cement block near the sidewalk."

"This rogue vampire wanted her to be found," Kim said, stating the obvious, just so they could fit the pieces together. "He really isn't doing this for pure pleasure."

"I kind of wonder," Jeremy continued in his bass voice, "why this vampire didn't leave Dar in the club like he did with most of the other drained victims."

"And why he attacked a woman in a nearby alley the time before that," Troy said.

Kim's eyes met Stephen's, and she knew exactly what he was thinking. Not because of some weird hypnosis, but because… Why? Did they have some deep connection or something? Hardly. She didn't know him at all—not beyond the sexual, anyway.

The thought felt hollow, leaving an echo in its wake. It rattled her for some reason—something she, once again, couldn't put her finger on.

She pulled her gaze away from the vampire's, more out of self-preservation than anything, then said what had to be on both of their minds. "The rogue is changing his game. It's almost like everything he's been doing until this point hasn't been getting him what he wants." She sighed. "If we only knew what *that* was."

When Stephen spoke up, the boys started, as if forgetting he was there. But Kim hadn't forgotten. Not for a second.

"Perhaps he *wishes* to get caught."

Troy just stared at Stephen.

Jeremy looked as taken aback by the stranger's British accent as much as by the statement itself. His mouth formed into an *O* as Kim shot Stephen a please-fade-into-the-background glare. Any revealed vampiness would only complicate things tonight, and she didn't have the time or inclination to deal with the fallout.

But, upon closer look, Stephen seemed so casual, so at home, that she was almost fooled, too. How would they ever guess what he was?

For a moment, her blood raced, and she couldn't help but wonder, what had he been like as a human? How old was he, anyway?

How had he become a vampire?

She wished she knew, wished she'd known what he was like before—

Wait. Why was she getting deep here? What did pillow talk have to do with getting the rush that only his bite provided?

As she focused back on Jeremy and Troy, she wondered briefly why she didn't just *tell* them that she had their Holy Grail right here—that this was a vampire, for heaven's sake. Shouldn't she be chomping at the bit to do that?

So why the hell didn't she?

"Listen," Troy finally said, his gaze lingering on Stephen as he addressed his cohorts. "Jeremy needs to get home before his mom puts out an all-points bulletin, and I'm sure, Kim, that you want to continue your *date*."

Jeremy lifted his eyebrows at the protective tenor of that last word. Kim dismissed it altogether.

"I'll spell Powder at Darlene's bedside later," their leader added, "after I've worked the phones to see if I can get any more info about what happened."

Troy had a few contacts on the cop front and, though Jeremy's parents were liberal with the curfew, he still answered to them.

But her? Who did she have to talk to now?

She definitely had one idea.

Before that vague sense of alienation could get to her,

Kim darted a glance to the exit, indicating to Stephen that they'd be continuing this "date" at a certain spot, no doubt, cordoned off by yellow crime-scene tape. Troy would have a mooing cow if he knew what she was planning, so she didn't tell him.

"I'll check in with you all later." She patted both Jeremy and Troy on their arms while breezing past them toward Stephen, who had a strange smile on his face as he stared at something in Jeremy's direction.

When she looked back at the high schooler, she realized that Stephen had been checking out Jeremy's winged superhero T-shirt.

Once again, she understood just what the vampire was thinking, and she couldn't help appreciating the irony, too.

All the same, she dug her hand into her shoulder bag, keeping the holy water vial and crucifix near.

Just in case she needed it with her new partner, after all.

KIMBERLY DIDN'T have to invite Stephen into her car this time and, after getting inside, they both sat wordlessly for a long moment—until he deemed the time ripe for making his thoughts known.

"You're planning to inspect the construction site?"

"You bet."

Kimberly started the car, which carried the trace of a cherry-laced air freshener that bludgeoned his senses until he blocked it out. The Chevy purred, adding even more vibration to the top layer of his flesh.

As if it needed more sensation when he was around her.

When he settled in, facing forward, he caught sight of the wide, roomy car hood through the windshield with its missing wiper. Ghosts of the previous night, when he had bitten her for the second time, brushed through him. The images were as misty as memory, yet strong enough to stir him as he recalled her splayed beneath him, her pale skin exposed, kissed by moonlight and the scratch of his fangs.

He held back a shudder, his lateral incisors elongating before he willed them to recede. All the same, desire compressed his body until it quivered with the strain of being held back.

She continued speaking while guiding the vehicle out of the parking lot. "Even if there're cops still hanging around, I figure maybe you can do your vampire thing, like maybe getting some readings or what have you. Speaking of which, did you see anything in Darlene's mind?"

"No. She was too medicated, her thoughts a swamp."

"Crap."

Stephen cocked an eyebrow. "Tell me—*you* need to be at the scene because…"

"You really have to ask?" Kimberly's knuckles were white as she gripped the wheel. "My friend was attacked. Isn't that better than any reason?"

It seemed that her focus had gone from tracking vampires for a sexual thrill to a far more dangerous motivation. A possible vendetta that could get her killed.

Again, he knew that keeping a willful woman such as Kimberly away from what she wanted to do was impossible. So he recommitted himself to watching over her, lest she get herself hurt.

Stephen rested an arm on the back of the seat. How he had gotten himself into protecting a human during this mission, he had no idea. He had too many other matters to attend to.

His hand dangled near her bare shoulder, and it was all he could do to stop himself from caressing her skin. It was so firm, so young. He already knew its taste, and the mere thought of enjoying more set his juices to flowing.

As Kim took a corner and entered the freeway, her body shifted so her shoulder whisked against his fingers. A thousand volts seemed to zoom through Stephen, bringing his flesh to a rolling pucker.

When he heard her sharp intake of breath, he knew she felt it, as well.

He removed his arm from the seat and positioned himself nearer the door. Megaresorts and bright lights blurred as they sped past, but the rate of travel seemed very slow to a vampire who was used to moving so quickly.

"Stephen?" she asked.

He was not certain he could answer without sounding like a schoolboy whose voice was changing. In response, he made something like a grunt.

"I'm just wondering, and I promise, I won't put anything you tell me on the Web…" She glanced quickly at him. "You *can* do things like get readings from this construction site, right?"

"If I'm fortunate, I'll be able to discern another's presence. Our senses are heightened when we turn. We experience more keenly—smell, hearing, vision and the like."

"Is that why sunlight kills vampires? Because you're more susceptible to UV rays than we are?"

He would have to tread cautiously here, revealing what could possibly aid her in self-defense, but not much more. Exposing the secrets his kind held dear wasn't prudent.

Stephen hesitated, surprised that he was swayed enough to tell her anything about his lifestyle. But when he considered what it might be like to find her harmed by the rogue, a blade of awful emotion dragged through the center of him.

Impossible, he told himself. He didn't feel a thing for her.

"Sensitivity to sunlight is a vampire's poison," he said, not deigning to add that the same went for the subject in general—sensitivity in emotion, in feeling.

"And all the other legends and rumors?" she asked. "Does garlic repel you?"

"Yes."

"Okay. I guess I'd better start carrying some. I hate to have it stink up my purse, though, you know?"

He fought to contain a sneak-attack grin. Kimberly was a funny one. "The crucifix you used on me is sufficient to repel."

"I'm carrying a little stake, too, just so you know. It fits right into my bag."

"Convenient." It rankled that she felt the need to inform him that she was hauling around a deadly weapon, as if she wished to warn him off, just in case.

Yet, could he blame her? He was *vampyr*. He was lethal, and there were times when he even feared that he—a master of control—might not be able to contain himself around her.

Even now, the scent of her skin was easing into him, tempting him. The soft thud of her pulse wasn't helping, either. His fangs threatened to come out again and he wrestled them back.

"What else?" she asked. "Mirrors, film? Can you see yourself in them?"

"No."

"Do you shapeshift like Dracula did? You know—into a bat, mist, a wolf thingamajig…"

"No." Though he knew those types of creatures existed. However, Fegan's gang made it a habit to avoid closely associating with others unless they were near the family's territory or unless Fegan himself decided to go on a solo rampage to assuage his bloody appetites.

"I hate to be rude," she said, using one hand to fix her high ponytail while the other kept steering, "but how can your kind be killed?"

As he watched her dodgy driving skills, he again debated the wisdom of imparting this information. Stephen had no doubts he could overpower her if need be, yet what if she came into contact with the rogue and she didn't know what to do?

Sweet mercy.

His answer rushed out. "A stake through the heart, fire, decapitation... Those are options."

As she lifted her other hand to fret with her hair, he grabbed the wheel to steady the car. She smiled, shrugged and abandoned her ponytail for safer driving.

Mortals. Many of them had no idea how quickly the end could come. Yet...

He recalled what she had shown him in her mind about her sister. Kimberly knew how fragile life was. So why test death as she did?

"Then, you guys really aren't immortal at all," she said, unruffled. "You just have really long lives until someone kills you."

"Yes." He got back on his side of the car, too overwhelmed by her to trust himself.

"And how do you become—" she paused, shifted, then continued "—absolutely mortal again? Or can you?"

She had asked this last part so softly that a human would

not have heard it. He also detected something more disturbing in her words—something that dug at the area they called a heart. It was as if she were trying to unearth *his* without knowing what damage she was wreaking.

For a moment, he allowed himself to give in, to experience one flash of joy because she seemed to care about his answer. "I can return to a mortal state, Kimberly, but at great cost."

"What?"

He didn't respond. It was a path he didn't wish to travel. His family was all there was left for him, and speaking of the only way to become mortal again was near blasphemy.

She seemed to accept that she had gone too far in the asking.

Silence rent the space between them, making the air too loud, the passage of every second too piercingly felt. A pressure welled inside of him. An expanding throb, a tugging that made him wish to smile and weep at the same moment.

Just when he thought he couldn't bear any more of it, he hacked away from the emotion.

Yet he had made the mistake of indulging and, now, his usual unfeeling state was not enough.

Not enough.

Numbing himself, he said, "I'm content as I am. I can barely recall my human days. And what I do remember doesn't inspire me to return to them."

As the lie fell to ash on his tongue, he thought of hard work on the estate under the thumb of his human master; thought of the time his own brother had betrayed him; thought of how that had eventually sent him reeling into the orbit of Fegan, who had taken him into the gang and made him part of a family that had lasted where the mortal one had not.

Kimberly hadn't remarked on his last comment. Was she struggling with a vague battle, as well? Did she, perhaps, believe that him staying on his side and her staying on the human one was for the best?

After all, even *she* had to know that their flirtations, as diverting as they were, held no importance.

"That's pretty dark, Stephen," she finally said. "Still… You say you're content, but are you happy?"

He didn't answer because he feared both of them already knew what he would say.

Slumping ever so slightly, Kimberly steered the car off the 15 and onto a side road. Across the freeway, the white lights of the Marrakech Casino blazed in invitation against a black sky.

The building was also visible from the construction site, where a couple of police vehicles were parked. Kimberly drove to another side street and then pulled over.

They sat in the car for a moment. He wondered if she was searching for a way to close their conversation, but he sensed that perhaps she didn't know how to do it.

"Let's avoid any official entanglements," he said, instead, opening the passenger-side door.

She hesitated, then nodded, clearly giving up the last of the oddly intimate discussion. "It might be smart to stay on the opposite end of where those cops are. That'd still be close enough to where Darlene was dropped for you to sense your clues, right?"

"Perhaps." Previously, he hadn't been able to read anything from the Mystique nightclub because of all the energy, all the bodies distracting him. Even the alley where last night's woman had been attacked held too many influences, since it was near the Strip's foot traffic. But here? There were only a few remaining authorities guarding the scene.

And Kimberly.

Could he get his mind off of her long enough to focus?

As she slipped her oversized bag across her chest, turned on a tiny flashlight and walked ahead of him, he began to doubt his fortitude. He kept watching the grace of her hips, the way her faded jeans cupped her rear end, the slim curves of her waist. All the while, night played over her skin, and he imagined running his mouth over it, biting into it.

Just as he started to be taken over by his hunger, Kimberly halted, then dashed over to the skeleton of a building that was in its first stages of birth. She hid behind what looked to be a steel pillar and pointed a finger north, where two officials were talking to each other by the only cement block near the sidewalk.

When she widened her pale eyes at him, Stephen understood. It might have been where Darlene was propped up to be discovered.

Good tracking, he thought. Perhaps Kimberly was a very talented hunter and he should be keeping watch over her for more reasons than her own safety. There was his own to consider, as well.

He concentrated on the cement block, reaching out with his mind to the rogue who had been here merely hours ago. A twinge needled through him, and he jerked.

Familiar. A feeling he could not pinpoint. A flicker of...

Without warning, a breeze hushed down from above

them on the construction beams. Before either Stephen or Kimberly could look up, a voice, a whisper attacked.

"Stephen…"

It traveled on the wind like a jagged threat.

Whoever it was knew his name.

Stephen's vision locked onto a shadow that loomed above them like a bird of prey, coat spread wide.

Kimberly! he thought, darting forward to shield her body with his own.

But she had already speared something into the rafters, toward the intruder. Just as Stephen reached her, he heard the creature yelp. Then, with a sucking sound, it extracted something from itself and dropped it.

A wooden stake quivered, impaled in the ground.

Then, quicker than the glint of a blade, the creature zoomed downward.

No!

It spread its coat, descending in a moment that seemed so much longer than that. Thinking only of protecting Kimberly, Stephen zoomed up toward it, intending to intercept.

With a screech, the rogue dodged, flaring past Stephen toward…

Kimberly!

Stephen whipped about, desperately trying to beat the rogue before it got to her first.

But it already had.

Everything happened in a blink. Kimberly lashed out, kicking with a well-aimed crunch that made the creature stumble before recovering.

It was not enough, for the rogue effortlessly grabbed her by the neck, exposing it to his mouth as Kimberly froze.

"Stop or I tear into her!" the shadow said to Stephen.

Out of pure terror for what the rogue might do next, Stephen halted his attack in midair, hovering. The rogue wore what looked to be sunglasses, plus a hooded jacket under his coat, and he'd pulled it over his head to hide all features. His scent was masked by cologne and he was mentally shielded, keeping Stephen from reading anything about him.

"I needed you to come alone after most of those cops went on their way," the rogue whispered, as if attempting to disguise his voice. "*This* one wasn't meant to be here."

"Let her free," Stephen said. He should be going after the rogue, subduing him so he could transport the criminal back to Fegan for the creator's satisfaction. He should be asking why the rogue knew his name. But he couldn't do it with Kimberly in this position.

How had this happened?

Stephen could see Kimberly, visibly shaking. Now she was face-to-face with a vampire who was not so choosy about his bites, and Stephen was angry with her for being so stubborn, so reckless. Why had he allowed her to accompany him? Why?

The rogue was shaking his head, as if disappointed by this outcome. "I finally catch you and what happens? A human ruins it. A…*human.*"

The last word was steeped in something besides hatred, an emotion Stephen would not have expected from a criminal who preyed upon mortals. No, there was…sorrow?

"Let her loose, and we'll have our own meeting," Stephen said calmly, the opposite of what he was actually feeling.

In the background, his hearing picked up exclamations of surprise and the policemen radioing for backup.

Time, he was losing time.

The rogue spoke again in that broken voice. "I was depending on talking to you, Stephen, *reasoning* with you since I know what slows your own walk nowadays. It's all lackluster, isn't it? The passage of nights, the routine of surviving, the easiness and similarities of places and things. It's all…lifeless."

Stephen flinched, though he tried to hide it. How did this rogue know?

The other vampire tightened his hold on a still Kimberly. She was being so brave, so smart by not testing this mad creature.

"What will it take to get to Fegan?" the rogue asked. "What else shall I do, Stephen? Perhaps if I attacked someone close enough to his enforcer it would produce faster results."

"No!"

Stephen flew forward to stop the rogue, but it was too late.

Kimberly cried out, not in passion, but in pain. The rogue had struck like a viper, sinking his teeth into her. Then, just as if he had made his point and was done for the night, he shot away, cutting the air in a clean escape.

Stephen screeched to a hovering stop, then fell to the ground near a slumped Kimberly. He should have given chase to the rogue—it was his mission.

But he couldn't.

He touched his fingers to Kimberly's neck, beginning the healing process. Then, holding her tightly, he sped away from the site before the lawmen came upon them.

He had traded the rogue for her safety; yet, in this wounded moment, it seemed like the best bargain in existence.

8

Kim came to gradually, feeling the pressure of fingertips on her neck and a soreness that tore at the tender skin there.

As her eyes adjusted to the near darkness, she realized she was in an abandoned building, plaster and wood littering the floor as the night peered through a hole in a wall. The mild smell of must added to the sense of isolation. She prepared herself for the scuttle of little feet over the floor, but there was no sound other than her own uneven pulse.

As she moved her head to look at whoever was touching her, she found a shape blocking most of what vague light there was. Her breathing quickened.

The fingers trailed away from her throat, leaving burning patches from the lack of contact.

Stephen.

"I have done as much as possible," he said gruffly, "but your injury will take more time to fully heal."

Suddenly, it all came back to her—the shadow above them on the construction beams, the bite the creature had given her after taking her captive.

But, this time, it wasn't the kind of bite she'd been longing for.

What she'd always thought to be an intimate, incredible

experience had hurt, ripped. The brutal entry had made her shrink into herself in shock and agony.

She reached up to feel her wound—two punctures, crusted and sensitive. Wincing, she brushed her thumb to the other side of her neck, where Stephen's bite lingered.

"The rogue didn't drain me," she whispered, vocal cords strained. "It *was* the rogue, right?"

"It had to have been." Stephen rose away from her, removing himself to stand by the broken wall. "He left before any draining could occur. However, I'm certain he only planned to prevent me from giving chase, or perhaps to teach me a lesson about pursuing him further. You weren't meant to be one of his normal victims."

Propped on her elbows, Kim couldn't tear her eyes away from Stephen. Her heartbeat fluttered in his presence, part fear, part yearning. The sight of him nailed her, leaving a raw trail of warmth until her entire body throbbed like one connected, exposed wound.

Why was he still here and not out getting the rogue?

"It knew your name," she said.

The vampire's back was to her as he watched the night readying itself for the coming of dawn. It was still maybe a couple of hours away, but he looked about ready to fly off into the darkness, regardless.

"Stephen?" Gathering strength, Kim sat all the way up. "How did the rogue know?"

His shoulders lost their arrogant line, as if he'd blown out a held breath. "I don't know, Kimberly. Perhaps the rogue heard the local vampire community speak my name in regards to hunting him down. Perhaps…" He trailed off.

Her skin flushed. "I'm sorry you couldn't chase the rogue because you had to tend to me." She'd never considered herself a liability, not when she'd done everything a single girl living alone should be doing—judo and self-defense classes, always trying to be aware of what was around her while walking. But look what'd happened—she'd messed up their chance to vindicate Darlene, who was lying in a hospital. "It's my fault we didn't get that vamp."

Something like a low laugh sounded, but she wasn't sure.

"You heaved a stake at him," Stephen said. "And it hit him *somewhere*."

"Thanks to my softball days." Kim shrugged. "My dad used to brag about my pitching arm."

And Lori had been the grand-slam hitter way back when. Their father had compensated for a lack of any sons by making sure his girls were well versed in sports; Mom had taught them that you could still be feminine at the same time. Kim had looked to her big sister for how to keep it all together.

Kim swallowed a lump that was growing in her throat. "Luckily, I can still hit a target."

"Nevertheless, I would prefer to face the rogue alone in the future. He might be twice as dangerous now; an animal backed into a corner."

Still smarting from thoughts of Lori, Kim was stuck on the part where Stephen kept calling the rogue a *he*.

"How can you be sure it was male?"

Stephen glanced halfway over his shoulder, but didn't look directly at her in his thoughtful pose. "I can't be certain. Do you have reason to believe the rogue is female?"

"I'm just an equal opportunity hunter." Truly, she had no reasons, but why limit themselves to one gender? "Hey,

I don't know how old you are, but in this day and age, women can be as destructive as men."

A strange smile—more of a scowl—captured Stephen's expression before he glanced away. "Then, nothing has changed in this world."

The way he said it made her want to fire off a hundred questions: Had a woman hurt him personally? And just how had he been born into this life? Where? When?

But his soft voice interrupted, taking on an edge as he folded his hands behind his back and kept staring out the wall's hole.

"Did you get what you wished for tonight, Kimberly?" he asked. "Did you enjoy *this* bite?"

His words were like a quick slap, stinging way more than the force that'd been used to strike her.

He was comparing the bite she'd been trying to wheedle out of him to this rogue's attack. Anger swelled, pushing outward.

He continued. "Was tonight's bite romantic?"

"Stop it." Her voice came out as a wounded hiss.

"I'm curious, that is all. You wished for another bite and you received it."

"You know it wasn't the same." Why was he doing this?

She wished she could articulate just what she got out of *his* bites, but if she, herself, didn't understand what the attraction was, how could she explain? All she knew was that Stephen got to her in ways no man could. In ways this violent bite couldn't begin to, either.

He finally turned completely from the wall, his body pure shadow, looming like the silent threat of midnight. His green eyes gave off a sparked glow, banked but menacing. Kim's pulse beat in her neck, her eardrums.

"A vampire bites because he's a predator, Kimberly." A hint of white fang lit the darkness. "We aren't the stuff of daydreams."

"Then, tell me why I've never gotten such satisfaction when I'm with a human."

Stephen merely stared, obviously at a loss for words.

"Don't tell me I'm romanticizing your bite," she said, struggling to stand, her legs unstable, like ice left in the sun too long. Her entire body felt as if it were melting, then coming to a fast boil. "I'm not imagining what I feel with you. It's more than just physical. It's…"

She searched for a phrase.

Stephen watched, as if trying to comprehend.

Words spilled out before they even took shape in her mind. "When I'm with you, I *understand.* I don't need to ask any more questions. I think that, maybe, everything will end up turning out all right in the end." She paused. "But after each bite, real life happens again and all the questions won't stop coming."

"Questions. About what?"

Kim slid to the ground, her back finding the wood from a decimated chair frame to support her. Numb, she felt so numb.

"Lori," she said, closing her eyes, seeing her laughing sister on the backs of her lids. Watching Lori's strawberry-blond hair catch a Tennessee breeze in the old days.

When she opened her eyes, dampness blurred her vision. It turned Stephen and the darkness into one black-and-green shape, like a kaleidoscope's shards.

It was only when tears fell that he became clear again.

He'd ventured closer, his expression as collected as usual except for a slightly furrowed forehead.

"My big sister," Kim said, wiping her cheek against her shoulder. She didn't want him to see her crying. The time for crying should've ended a long time ago. "After her death, I lost faith in anything and everything. I lost hope, and sometimes I think you'll be the one who can…"

Give it back to her by detailing what it was like to pass from this life to another?

"Sister." Stephen said it as if testing the word.

Then, before Kim could react, he closed the distance between them, reaching out, placing his fingers on her temple so gently that it had all the weight of a butterfly.

It was as if he were asking to see what she was really thinking, to witness everything she found so impossible to express in words.

"Yes," she whispered, body going limp and warm as she felt a pleasant heaviness in her mind, as if something welcome had joined her there after she'd given it permission.

She pictured Lori again, laughing, lifting her face to the sun.

Seconds later, Stephen removed his fingers, the cold/warm imprint of them lingering and throbbing on her flesh even as the weight in her mind disappeared. She felt a keen loss—was it because he was gone?—and realized that he had joined with one of her memories in his own vampire way.

"I'm sorry, Kimberly," he said.

"For reading my thoughts? I was fine with that."

"No." He moved away, came to a plastic-covered sofa, then busied himself with taking off the tarp. It was as if someone had stopped in the middle of moving out the furniture, leaving only a stray piece here and there. "I'm sorry she's gone and…"

A slant of weak moonlight rotated through the hole in the wall to reveal Stephen staring into the distance, the glow robbed from his gaze.

"And?" Kim asked, wanting so badly to reconnect with whatever it was he had brought to her just now.

"And I understand. I could see what you might be searching for." He lowered himself to the sofa, looking defeated. "Yet I cannot give peace to you—not anything more than the specter of it, anyway."

Her posture slumped. His bite: The one thing that had infused her with hope, the one thing that maybe could've explained everything, and it wasn't real.

Yet… Dammit, she still wanted him to come to her again. It was all she had.

Sadness expanded until it became her voice. "I miss her so much. To this day, I worry about her and I can't stop."

"I know." He just kept looking at nothing. "Is she happy now that she's left this world? Or do they even exist in any form?"

Kim tilted her head. When had *she* turned to *they?*

The vampire seemed to catch on without her even having to ask. "I have seen loved ones leave, as well. When I was human, I lost my brother…."

He stopped, as if becoming just as confused as she was about all the questions.

"Your brother," she added, "you can't stop thinking about him, either?"

When their gazes met, she saw the same devastation she knew and it made things worse, not better. She'd always wanted to find someone who understood, but she didn't want them to feel as empty as she did.

Tears pushed at the backs of her eyes. Stephen really

didn't know the answers. And, if a creature who lived so close to death didn't, who did?

She broke into a sob and angrily tried to hold back. Yet the force of so much built-up sorrow overtook her, reducing her to silent tears that she tried to hide with all her might.

"Kimberly…" he whispered, his voice a balm, the very thing she needed, even though she knew it wasn't real. It was only a vampire trick, the seduction he'd used on others to get the blood he needed to survive.

But she found herself talking through the tears, relieving the burden she'd been carrying for more than a year now because there was no other way to cope.

"We said we'd always be together." Kim twined her fingers together, staring at them through a blur. "Sisters. But she *left* me. And my parents… They're like ghosts. I feel like they're not even there anymore, either."

"Everyone needs family, to have someone else," Stephen said. "Everyone."

He'd said it with such wistfulness that Kim held her breath and watched him, her own sadness suspended.

A bite. It was the only thing that had made her feel vital in so long. It would make her feel so much better now, even if it was just a fantasy.

As if sensing her need, Stephen stiffened.

"I saw many things in your mind," he said, as if trying to steer clear of what she was gearing up to get from him. "Not only did you lose your sister, but her child, as well. Although Lori was only a month and a half along, you had already started buying toys for your niece or nephew."

Kim shied backward, spine against the chair wood. It wasn't so much that he'd read this from her—it was that the naked truth burned.

"I saw that you used to want children, too," Stephen added.

She tried to play it off, as if what he said was in the past and therefore sterile. "I used to. Believe it or not, I used to think I was a normal woman who just wanted a husband and family. But after our first…encounter…I rethought all of that. I became someone else entirely—a person who didn't need those kinds of ties because she knew they could disappear in an awful second."

Stephen narrowed his eyes in perception. "But sometimes you miss what you used to want, like children. Sometimes you wonder if you can ever go back to feeling that way, and then you remember the anguish of losing."

Stunned by his precision, she sat there, anesthetized. Then a yearning crept over her, as if let out of its cage. It begged to allow in what she'd denied herself after Lori and her child had died.

Sending him a pleading glance, she said, "I'm so scared to want the same things. I'm scared of seeing them disappear before I even have them, so I changed my needs and told myself I'd never have to deal with the devastation."

Now I want what's much easier to get, she thought. Sex had tided her over for so long that she'd convinced herself it was all there was.

But Stephen had reminded her otherwise, even as he fulfilled her simpler needs.

When he took her hand in his, his skin was cool, otherworldly. It made her want to cry again, because merely touching him wasn't going to solve anything.

She knew that without a doubt now.

As KIMBERLY LOWERED her head and hid her face from Stephen, he didn't force the issue. He could not stand to watch her cry, and he was thankful her sorrow was not in full view.

He could not afford to empathize with it.

Still, her naked emotion touched him. He had no idea his bite could mean so much to one of them. It had always been just a means to a meal, a necessity. Yet, it was only now, in the net of her tears, that he realized he had the potential to have wreaked this sort of personal damage on every woman he had seduced into giving blood. In his detached state of being, he had refused to even consider that.

While Kimberly fought her tears, Stephen's chest felt pried open, his heart exposed and prodded to sharp sensation. He didn't know how to comfort her, though his instincts screeched at him to try.

He had brought a measure of this upon her, and he was compelled to alleviate it. After all, he had spent years robbing and his crimes had crept into his consciousness over the decades, making him less and less comfortable with his lifestyle, though he didn't know how else to carry through the years.

But how? How could he bring her comfort short of the bite she coveted?

Earlier, Kimberly's eyes had gleamed with something like hope when he had mentioned his younger brother, and he knew just how much her sister's death hurt her—when she had given him permission to enter her mind, that was all he had seen. Thoughts of this Lori drove her, darkened her.

Shouldn't he attempt to soothe her by commiserating about his own losses?

He dredged up Nathan's face, but it was muddled by the passage of time. So many faces, decade by decade, century by century. Even those he had loved had faded like portraits veiled by dust and left untended.

Holding her hand, he hesitated one more moment, reluctance getting the better of him. In the corner, a rat stuck its head out of a tunneled hole. Stephen silently commanded it to leave, just as he had done with the rest of the creatures when he had brought Kimberly here to rest.

To rest, he thought. To heal.

"His name was Nathan," Stephen finally said.

Kimberly froze, as if attempting to decode what language he was speaking. Then she sniffed back her sadness, her grip tightening around his hand. She was so warm, so fragrant and tempting, her tears bringing out a purity not unlike petals washed by rain.

His blood quickened, but he stilled his urges.

"Nathan?" she asked.

"As a human," he said, "I was born in the early eighteenth century on a manor well outside of London, the first son of servants. My parents expired..." The word seemed wrong, absent of the emotion he had felt as a young man, so he made another attempt. "My parents died in an overturned coach as they traveled to pay respects to an elderly aunt I had never met."

Pausing, he saw that she had pushed a stray lock of red hair from her face, revealing tear-stained pale skin that he yearned to caress. Yet, it wasn't out of passion— not entirely. He wished to lay a palm to her cheek because it might quell the unnerving, unnameable emotion these memories were stirring—memories unexplored since his choice to turn away from humanity all those years ago.

"Were you young when it happened?" she asked. "I

can't imagine being orphaned even now, when I'm supposed to be this adult who can handle it."

"I was…" Stephen was surprised to realize he didn't recall how old he had been. He merely had a distant feeling of it being much too early to lose the people whom he had looked up to and loved.

"It's okay." Kimberly clasped his hand tighter.

She seemed to know that he was finding it difficult to piece together his crumbled past. He slid his fingers farther over her hand, encompassing her in his grip and thinking it was nice.

He added, "The master of the manor accepted responsibility for Nathan and me, yet I was a proud one. I wouldn't have any part of his kindness. Besides, I dreamed of London and what the streets held for a young man with ambitions. I believed I could earn my way with perhaps an apprenticeship and then my own shop. A smithy, since I was versed in the trade on the estate."

"You didn't want to be a charity case," she said.

Her tears had subsided. His instincts sent up a red flag: *Stop! Your job is done! Leave!*

Yet he continued, anyway, and he suspected that it was because this felt nice, too. This easy unburdening.

"Nathan had refused to accompany me to London, but I'd assured him I would return when I had become a success. I'd been determined to keep what family I'd had together, without the pity of anyone else to maintain us. So I'd made my way to the city, apprenticing at a smithy, then eventually opening my own shop. But I was always catching up financially, never stable enough to be able to take in Nathan."

"You had to leave him behind?"

"At that point, I was not going to allow that to happen. No, I…" A combination of shame and excitement bolted through him. "I found another way to earn my coin."

Kimberly gave him a sidelong gaze and, suddenly, the days—the nights—were back upon him. A lovely lady peeking out from the shade of a coach as he pointed a pistol at her father or husband and told him to stand and deliver.

Stephen couldn't hold back a bitter grin. "I took to robbing the roads."

A beat passed as Kimberly absorbed that. She was, no doubt, remembering when he had told her to stand and deliver the other night. He hadn't left *all* of his past behind—just the parts that were too impossible to maintain.

"You were a…highwayman?" she asked, smiling in disbelief.

Even as a tweak of remorse got to him, his blood gave a jolt. He was once a "thrill seeker" and, even now, it appealed, mainly because his tale had dashed away Kimberly's sadness.

"I started later than most gentleman robbers, yet lived longer than many due to unexpected circumstances." In other words, Fegan.

Kimberly was still watching him closely. "From a mild-mannered smith to a dashing highwayman."

Again, she was romanticizing when she shouldn't be. Before he could correct her, however, she continued, "I know what it's like to find a new angle of personality. Believe me."

He thought of her reclining against the windshield of the Chevy, skin bared, breasts heavy and red-tipped.

His gums tingled as his fangs threatened.

"A highwayman," she said.

He shouldn't be so happy that she found him this irresistible.

Kimberly gripped his hand harder. Her skin had grown moist, her pale blue eyes wide. "Did your brother join you then?"

"No. When I'd approached him about leaving the manor, my pockets weighed with gold, he'd refused. By then he'd been a young buck in love and enjoying country life as it was, although he would have had to serve a master until the end. I'd been angry at the rejection, and I'd returned to robbing with a vengeance, as if that would prove to Nathan that he had chosen wrong."

"I'm sure you got a nasty reputation."

The Gray Phantom. That was what they had called him, the masked robber who roamed the roads like mist and had never gotten caught by the authorities. Yet he didn't reveal this to her. Stoking her fire wouldn't be wise at all.

For her *nor* him.

"But what about the vampire part?" Kimberly's flushed skin spoke of her growing stimulation.

Perhaps the story should end here. Yet he found himself so enamored of her excitement that he couldn't refrain; he would put an end to this soon. He could control the situation.

"Though I'd escaped the law, time and again, I was becoming careless." That was an understatement. He had stopped caring altogether, feeling too alone and wondering why he continued to gather riches when Nathan would never require them. "A man—actually a vampire—named Fegan had a gang who moved into my territory. Soon, I discovered they weren't so much interested in my loot as they were in recruiting me into their ranks. And I'd been very willing."

Cursed to a life of hiding and isolation, he had missed Nathan, missed his parents. It'd made him all too vulnerable to the glamour of vampire togetherness, promises of jolly relationships that would last and last. "He turned me, then gave me a family again. We hid in a forest cave by day, then emerged by night to steal money, valuables and blood from our prey."

"Still, you never got caught."

If there were any justice in this world, he should have gotten caught at some point. Why hadn't he?

"No, luv. There were close calls, but we never did."

Her pulse was thudding against her skin, echoing into his own flesh and wiping out all other thought. He welcomed that, needed that, because with the awakening of his emotions came the remorse, as well.

He had robbed, gotten off scot-free…

He embraced how his body was overriding his mind. His pulse matched her own, linking them in a primal rhythm.

"What came next?" she asked, breathless. "Tell me, Stephen."

He didn't even think twice now, not if he wanted to chase away this newly emerged guilt.

It felt too good to surrender.

"After highway robbery became less lucrative," he said, "the gang moved on, always lingering on the shady side of deals, no matter where we settled in the world."

"Where'd you go? Europe, Asia…"

"Mostly the continent, yet we couldn't resist America, the land of opportunity. We avoided the War between the States, then profited from Reconstruction."

That had been Fegan's idea, and Stephen had gladly traveled overseas with the gang. Back then, before Cassandra, he had thrived on pleasing his new father, found contentment in helping to keep his vampire family comfortable.

Odd how his relationship with Fegan actually echoed the one he had with his mortal parent, and even with the Lord of the manor. Stephen had been somewhat of a "black sheep" in those cases—too stubborn to be anything like the perfect son. The same had come true with Fegan, validating a pattern that followed Stephen no matter who he was or what he had become.

"What happened next?" Kimberly asked.

Suddenly, a light seemed to dim over her, obscuring her features, but he knew it was only in his mind. Cassandra Danforth, the belle of Savannah. The woman Stephen had loved by moonlight only to be rejected in the end.

One night had changed everything—the time he had lost control and his fangs had sprouted during the heat of the moment. After witnessing her horror, he had become resentful of what he was, too self-aware of what he lacked in humanity. He had become so aware, in fact, that he had forced himself to purge any remnants, any ties to it. He had become all monster, dedicated to survival even as he abhorred it.

His self-disgust had extended to his bond with Fegan, who couldn't understand Stephen's attitude. Their strained father-son ties had all but snapped; Fegan wondering how a son of his could be bored with this existence. Wondering how that boredom could have ever grown from the realization that they could possess everything, that there was no longer anything to look forward to.

Stephen's disillusionment had spread to other gang

members: "Lucky" Diggory, a street rat, who had carelessly allowed humans to stake him during a trip to New Orleans. Edward Marburn, the wrong-side-of-the-blankets son of a titled father, who had left the gang during the Second World War. And Thomas Kincaid, a poet, who had gladly surrendered himself to a terrified mob in Bucharest after they had found him feeding.

Yet Stephen had stayed with the family through it all. They were not going to leave *him* this time. He was never going to let them go.

A tug on his hand brought him back to the moment. Kimberly's face cleared in his vision—the beautiful, delicate features that reminded him of a woodland pixie, the bold red hair, the parted lips that had brought him so much pleasure.

The woman who had actually sought out and reveled in his bite.

His perception crashed around him, like fragments of mirror warping his vision with different angles of view. He could not see the truth anymore—could not put together a whole picture.

"Stephen?" she asked. "Tell me more."

He knew that he had primed her with mere words, with the promise of fantasy.

She wanted him, the vampire, and, though part of him despised that, part of him was overcome.

As his fangs elongated, he looked into her eyes. She was willing, allowing him to come into her, to fuse with her own thoughts.

Unable to fight himself any longer, he captivated her mind, giving both of them what they hungered for.

9

He PAINTED a picture in her mind, knowing exactly what she wanted—dark woods, looming trees whispering in the wind, the clatter of a team of horses as they pulled a grumbling coach over the rough road.

Then, as if caressing her with an artist's brush, he clothed her fantasy self in a gown of dove-gray silk, a matching hooded cape. Her upswept hair was powdered, as the fashion of the day dictated. Around her neck she wore a strand of diamonds that set off her delectable throat, so pale in the moonlight nudging through the coach's window as she opened the curtain a slit, curious about what lay outside.

No woman of her station would have been traveling the dark woods unescorted, but this was a fantasy. Hers.

Theirs.

As the clatter of the coach and horses consumed him, Stephen impulsively embraced the resurging sensations: The thrust of adrenaline, the devil-may-care eagerness of a coming robbery. He had not realized how much he missed the thrill of darkness and road, the anticipation of what was going to happen next.

"You are a lady," Stephen whispered, readying her. "A young insatiable one who is bored and spoiled with the abundance in your family's coffers."

In dreamlike time, she smiled, and he knew she would be doing the same in reality.

Carried away, he continued, body heat rising in near fever, in remembrance of how it used to be as a human who had gone from good man to bad. "You are returning much too late from a ball in town. If you are caught tiptoeing into the mansion at this hour by your family, you will, no doubt, be punished."

Fantasy Kimberly closed the curtain and leaned back in her seat, languid. She was a wanton who didn't mind chastisement, for she would only tiptoe out the next night and do the same wicked things.

Stephen's pulse banged, much like it had way back when, while he waited for coaches to approach on those wooded roads. His veins were taut, like vibrating wire stringing his body together.

It was as if he had been fully transported to a wonderfully mortal moment now, sitting casually on his mount while his blood punched its way to his skin. He was wearing a half-mask to shroud his features, a tricorne and a cloak. In his hand, he held a pistol.

When the coach rumbled around a corner, Stephen urged his horse forward, raising his weapon.

The driver, no fool, brought his horses to a halt, understanding the message a pistol presented. There were no footmen, no escorts to contend with. No, the lady inside the coach had attempted to remain discreet tonight.

The convenience made the fantasy much smoother.

With a wave of his pistol, Stephen persuaded the driver to alight from his perch. Then, with nary a spoken command, he signaled that the poor wretch strip to his underthings.

"Sorry, my friend," Stephen said, dismounting, tying the shivering man's wrists and ankles together, then positioning him on the side of the road. Out of a stray sense of pity, he draped the driver's coat over the man's shoulders.

With a tip of his hat, he returned to the coach, heartbeat booming like a cannon.

At the conveyance's door, he raised his pistol, grinned, then opened up.

And there she was, hand to her swelling breast, hood slumped away from her powdered hair, lips parted in anticipation.

"Hello, m'lady," he murmured. "How fared the festivities?"

She was almost panting at his appearance. "I'm sure they weren't half as interesting as this."

The combination of Kimberly's anachronistic speech and sexy throwback apparel drove him on—especially since he knew what lay beneath both her cheeky words *and* her skirts.

No turning back now, he thought, feeling every last vestige of doubt slipping away. *Worry later about the consequences of what you're allowing to happen.*

There. He felt light, happy...*new.*

"Well, luv." He leaned against the doorframe, still training his pistol just off target. "Surely, you know these woods are dangerous. Only the brave ride at this time of night."

The jeweled necklace gleamed. To the human Stephen, its riches would have represented such hope, such a promise to finally bring his brother to live with him in comfort, had Nathan the desire to do so.

Now it was more a reflection of Kimberly's pale eyes as they glittered in the moonlight with playful abandon.

The highwayman came back to Stephen all too easily as he thought, *This one isn't as afraid as she should be.*

It amused him even while keeping him on edge. "Perhaps," he said, "you're waiting to remove that bauble until I speak the magic words?"

Laughing softly, Kimberly relaxed on the plush cushions, resting on a hip and sliding over until she leaned her elbow on the back of the seat and propped up her head.

"What words would those be?" she asked lazily.

His body stiffened, just as it would have if he were still mortal…gloriously mortal. To complete the fantasy, he strained against his trousers, feeling the tip of his cock beading with slight fluid—a secretion that would be potent, unlike a vampire's.

Stephen lowered his voice to a midnight scratch. "Stand and deliver, luv."

It seemed to be just what she had been waiting for. Yet, instead of moving to appease him, she merely sank farther into her naughty pose. Moonlight revealed her ripe breasts almost spilling out of her décolletage, the tips peeking out as her breathing came faster.

"I believe, I'll make you work for it," she said.

Even in human form, Stephen had been athletic and skillful, so in this fantasy he dove into the coach before she could react, threatening without carrying through on any dark promises.

Yet.

He sat on the opposite side, legs splayed before him while resting his arms on the back of the seat. His pistol dangled, belying its readiness.

Free, he thought. *So many years and only now do I finally feel free.*

"Really, m'lady. Consider divesting yourself of that necklace. Help out a hardworking lad."

"And what would I get in return?"

Minx. Pressure seemed to be expanding his cock into one pounding distraction.

"I suppose," he said negligently, "your reward will have to remain a surprise until you earn it."

Her smile growing wider, she moved forward in her seat, her skirts rustling. When she reached behind to undo the necklace, her breasts swelled even more, and saliva flooded Stephen's mouth, stinging his jaws.

"Hmm." Flummoxed, she raised her empty hands in a mock helpless gesture. "I'm having some trouble here. It's the clasp. No wonder I'd need a maid to help me dress."

Her modern sense of humor sent Stephen's thoughts into chaos. He was not even certain whether he was reliving his humanity or being guided by her own fantasies.

This had never happened before; he had always been the one to lead the hypnosis. How—

When she turned her back to him, presenting a long, graceful nape, his thoughts blanked out. Almost worshipfully, he ran his fingers from her hairline down her spine, stopping at the bump where the necklace rested. Goose bumps rose over her skin.

Her flesh gave off an intoxicating scent—purity, musk, the perfume of the living….

Feral need rose inside him, destroying the fantasy as it was.

Vision going red, he tore at the clasp. The necklace broke, falling piecemeal to the floor like diamond drops of rain. Kimberly gasped and reached for a descending gem, but Stephen had lost all restraint by now, his dream-inspired humanity destroyed with just the hint of dizzying blood that was pumping under her skin.

His fangs grew sharp and long, his throat tightening in horror, in disappointment, in self-disgust.

He was *vampyr,* fantasy or not.

But his roughness seemed to kick the blood through her at an even hotter rate. She leaned her head back, offering her neck to him.

"Do it, Stephen. *Do it.*"

He was almost beyond resisting; only a tremble of self-control held him back.

Yet, even that disappeared in the next heartbeat. He dropped the pistol and moved his hands around to her front, putting all his rage into tearing the bodice from her chest.

The rip was like thunder in the confines of the coach, her intake of breath sharp enough to abrade his nerve endings. Mouth watering, Stephen bent her back so that she was lying on his lap, her head resting on his coach seat. Locks fell from her neat, upswept style as her eyes widened, pupils eclipsing her irises.

His attention traveled down to her naked breasts, round and creamy and painted by the moon. The deep red tips of them puckered under his hungry gaze.

He pulled her up to him, arching her back as he fixed his mouth to one of those nipples. He sucked at her, tonguing her and devouring her until she winced and knocked the tricorne off his head while grabbing his hair. Meanwhile, he kneaded her other breast, unable to get enough of its fullness, its warmth.

A stray thought from her mind invaded his own: *Just like* Tom Jones...

He mentally swiped that aside. To him, this was real. But

the parallel unreality of it kept him safe from what he usually forbade himself to do outside of fantasy. Here, in her mind, could he love her, taste her, even…bite her again?

Shaken, he buried his face between her breasts, catching his breath, his sanity.

"Don't you dare stop," Kimberly panted, pulling his hair and forcing him upward.

A false romp, he thought. That is all this is.

He pushed her skirts up, feeling silken stockings, garters and…nothing else. Should he be surprised that he had given Kimberly no underclothing in this dreamscape?

Not really—not when there was a driver outside who probably would have been causing trouble by now, had this been reality. Not when there were no other gang members to watch his back as he took his leisurely time in here.

He brushed his fingers against the center of her legs, feeling a thatch of downy hair, then the drenched heat of her need.

Wet, he thought. *Ready for me.*

With her skirts around her hips, he turned both their bodies so that they stretched over the cushions. Then he tugged her legs so that she could clasp them around his hips. In an inspired touch, he drove his cock against her, teasing her just to be cruel.

"Pants…off," she said, grinding against him in an equally furious response.

Laughing, he stilled her hips, then slowly taunted her with his tip. Even through his trousers, he could feel himself sliding up and down her slick crevice.

Blood thundered into his penis, buffeting and demanding to set something loose.

"Be that way, then," she said, moaning and laughing,

too, then reaching back between his legs to brush beneath his balls.

With a grunt of pleasure, he pushed right back against her sex, thrusting again, then again until she groaned.

Soon, they caught a rhythm. The coach's springs moaned as he played with her, drove her to a frustrated cry.

"Now," she yelled, pushing down his head and guiding his mouth to her neck.

The scent of her, the heat—

He sank his fangs into her jugular. She pulled at his cloak, bucking against him and wincing. Though he soothed her with his mind, sedating her, she seemed to embrace the pain, embrace everything his bite obviously gave to her.

This woman who wasn't afraid of his true face, this woman who couldn't be pushed away with what he truly was…

Then his sight went dizzy and white. How? Why?

As her blood filled his mouth, sending a shock through him, he came, shooting hot and wet against his trousers, spilling in violent spurts. But he was not famished for her blood so much as for *her*—the spirit of the woman, the essence.

White…

…life…

…white…feeling…

…pain…white…pleasure…*alive*—

A cry ripped from her throat at the same time it did his. With one long yank at his cloak, she stiffened against him, rocking upward as if seeking the skies.

As their climaxes crashed, they both gripped something besides each other. She grasped his coat while clamoring for breath. He clutched the seat cushions until the stuffing bulged out of them, his fangs finding his own lips, his own blood.

Feeling…

…alive…

Slowly, very slowly, the real world dimmed into focus.

He was lying on top of her on the couch in the abandoned building. The smell of the nearby city's thick, polluted air shook him out of his trance, and he backed away while keeping his healing fingers to her neck, where the tattoo-covered evidence of this latest bite.

Something he barely remembered doing.

As the punctures began to close up with expedient efficiency, her heartbeat evened out.

He kept staring at that bite, avoiding her searching gaze. *I did it again,* he thought. *I couldn't stop.*

His gaze wandered. Where she would have worn a gown's bodice, her tank top and bra were now torn, exposing her perspiration-gleamed breasts. Her jeans were sticky with his juices; the sight of that clutched at him because even though he had come against her, there was no life to his seed.

Just as there could be no life outside of the completed fantasy, either.

KIM'S GAZE began to adjust out of its scrambled puzzle, but she didn't want to leave the beauty of what she'd just experienced. Not yet.

Had it really happened? Had Stephen given her the most shattering orgasm of her life?

She wanted to return to the coach, to the silk gown and diamond necklace, to the highway robber who'd seduced her. After Stephen had told her his history, she'd been his—ready and willing. His life story had turned her on.

But there'd been something about the telling itself, as if a lot of pain had been etched into what he wasn't revealing. It was as if even more of his tale had been left in the white spaces, the "gutters" that separated panels of a comic book and forced the reader to fill in the blanks.

The mystery of him thrilled through her again. Stephen, the enigma.

Absently, while her eyes were still mist-filled, her body still lazy with pulsating warmth, she skimmed a hand to the wetness between her legs. Evidence of what was hers *and* his.

She'd made him explode, too.

Sliding her other hand up to her neck, she felt the tender, sore skin. Her adrenaline gathered, then flooded every inch below her skin.

Another bite.

She'd cried out for it, wanting with all her soul to be the best he'd ever had, knowing it would somehow matter. But she could feel the completeness of the bite seeping out of her like spent blood.

She couldn't hold on to the feeling.

Why? Was something missing? What would make her happy beyond what had just happened? What would really make this a definitive connection?

She didn't know. But as the swirling afterglow released her from its grasp, reality set in. Suspicions about how she could feel so full, yet so hollow at the same time.

When her eyes focused, she found Stephen leaning against a paint-chipped wall. The light that angled over him was a predawn tweak that signaled the passing of night. He wouldn't be staying for much longer at all.

Her heart dropped, and that surprised her. Her heart shouldn't have anything to do with this.

Getting herself together, she smiled at him, and he returned the gesture.

"Wow," she said.

A beat passed, awkward yet intimate. He raised an eyebrow, still too mysterious for his own good, even though she thought he looked pretty damned satisfied, himself.

But he also looked…regretful.

Kim struggled to sit up, and her head swam.

"I stopped drinking before I took too much blood from you," he said. "I was not hungry so much as…"

It was beyond her to supply him with a description. She couldn't think of much to say, either. Maybe he had fed off of something else besides blood tonight; she'd gotten a hint of that during their second bite, on the hood of the Chevy. It'd been as if he'd been sustaining himself with a psychic quality. She'd read about vampires who did that—drew off human energy and not blood. Maybe Stephen needed both.

He looked away from her. "Before now, I've only needed blood."

She was afraid to say it. "I'm giving you something besides that?"

As he met her gaze, her body felt like metal sheeting hit by a hammer.

His intensity was almost unbearable. "I have never remembered what it was like to be human as I do when I am with you. I take *that* from you, Kimberly. Somehow, you provide it for me when no one else does."

His admission startled her. Suddenly, she felt uncovered, nude, but in a mental way.

God. She couldn't care less when he fed off of her blood, but this was something more personal, more valuable.

But shouldn't she be jumping for joy? He'd just told her she wasn't like the others.

No. It actually felt…empty. Maybe because she wasn't willing to accept it and see where it could lead. This went beyond easy sex, easy blood-giving.

At her reaction, a sad smile captured his lips. "I understand."

She donned her flirty shield, the defenses she'd plated over her skin after Lori had died. That was a part of what had happened, right? The first bite had allowed her to become someone different, someone who didn't allow any man under her skin because he could never match what a vampire had given to her. *Life* could never match it.

But now that her vampire was here, she was still steely.

Who the hell was she, anymore?

He added, "I see how it is, Kimberly, how it has to be."

"What do you—"

He held up a hand, putting an end to the conversation.

What had he been trying to tell her? It was as if he'd started to spill his heart out but had cut himself off. Why?

Even while she was asking, she knew it was for the best. They had more to do than sort out human-vampire relations issues. He was just a bite to her, and she was…

Good God, she really was more to him.

Once again, she thought of what this last bite had been lacking. Whatever it was, deep down, she really did want it, knew it was the only thing that could satisfy her.

But she was afraid. So damned afraid.

As the light shifted ever so slightly, Stephen sighed, moving away from the wall with the fluid grace that held her so enthralled. A gust of wind flapped at his long coat.

"I need to leave."

Her response was out of her mouth before she could censure it. "I wish you wouldn't."

He seemed surprised by her heartfelt reaction and, for a moment, it looked as if he didn't know what to do about it. Then he went back to being the unruffled vampire who'd captured her imagination, even though she knew there was more to him.

"Though I can always 'hole up' in a dark, hidden place," he said, "I prefer my comforts, my family."

"Your family," she repeated wonderingly. "Not your brother…"

"No." Stephen's posture went ramrod straight. "My brother passed on long ago while still a mortal."

When he glanced at her, she saw that he understood what she'd been through with Lori. He sympathized with the loss.

"Are we all bound to disappoint you?" she whispered. Maybe she shouldn't have said it, but it was in her heart. She didn't like realizing that.

He opened his mouth, but, instead of uttering something, he went into vampire mode, darting at her with such speed that she barely had time to gasp before she realized he'd cocooned her in his coat and was speeding through the night.

Just as quickly, she found herself inside her Chevy near the construction site, dizzy as a slight wind whipped past her.

Too late, she realized that breeze had only been Stephen leaving her alone.

But she was used to that feeling.

A FEW DESERT MILES AWAY, in an abandoned gas station, the rogue burrowed beneath some blankets in an old, rusted semitrailer. At the threat of every dawn, he locked it from the inside, as he'd rigged it to do. No human would have the strength to get past the door unless they made a lot of alarming noise.

In the peaceful darkness of the trailer, he tried to forget what a disaster the night had turned out to be. It had started well enough with the attack on the woman—a member of a vampire-hunting organization called the Van Helsing League. Her picture had been on their Internet site, bold as you please, and her intention to "patrol" Mystique was plainly posted in one of the site's columns.

Humans. So arrogant in their naiveté. Hadn't they ever stopped to think that a real vampire could keep tabs on them?

This Darlene he had attacked was a perfect victim, an ideal choice for gaining the attention he needed. And his plan had worked to a certain extent. Through listening to the whispers of other local vampires who didn't realize he was eavesdropping while they roamed casinos and bars, the rogue knew that Stephen Cole had been assigned to track him down.

And that Stephen Cole had been using the aid of this Van Helsing League to do it.

Well, track him Stephen had, just as the rogue wanted. And if things had gone according to plan, Stephen would have led him to Fegan, the most powerful master in the area.

The rogue only wished one of those human hunters hadn't been with Stephen tonight.

He yanked at a blanket. He hadn't expected her. He also hadn't anticipated her throwing a stake at his arm. Even now, the almost-healed wound nagged a bit, exacerbating his usually mild temper.

Cursed hunter. At the construction site, where he'd left Darlene to lure Stephen into the private conversation all the previous drainings had been leading up to, the rogue's senses had been filled with the human scent of the cops; this had distracted him from honing in on the hunter until it was too late. Seeing her, he'd thought quickly, hoping to get Stephen to perhaps hear him out while using the redhead as a shield from an attack. The rogue hadn't wanted to bite her, but it had been necessary when Stephen overreacted.

That had surprised the rogue the most, really. Stephen's possessive response.

The rogue settled on his back, covered by the blankets except for his mouth, his breathing slowing as rest descended.

Tonight his plans to be peacefully taken to the wisely hidden Fegan hadn't worked. He'd been close—excruciatingly close—and now all he could do was wait for tonight's seeds to flower. Always careful, he had put a backup plan into motion that would definitely bring Stephen to him again—but on the rogue's terms.

For Stephen Cole *would* understand.

He would help him get to Fegan, the only vampire who could give the rogue what he was searching for.

10

MORNING SOON glimpsed over the mountains, layering gradual strokes of orange and purple over the sky as day gathered strength.

Kim was sitting in the front seat of her idling Chevy, holding her cell phone and playing with the fringes of the blanket over her shoulders. It was from the backseat, and just after Stephen had left, she'd realized that he'd draped it over her.

Nice that he'd thought to do that.

The phone was the second thing she'd grabbed out of her purse after Stephen had secured her in the car. The first item had been a crucifix, which she'd hung around her neck. Even though dawn had emerged shortly after Stephen had left, Kim felt a chill near the construction site where her car was parked, so she'd taken precautions.

After all, this was where the rogue had taken Darlene, where the rogue had bitten *Kim* last night. If Stephen hadn't reacted so quickly to chase the bad vamp away then heal her....

Stephen. She let the name slide through her. It was like drinking a potion that warmed her from belly to limbs.

As she glanced outside her Chevy, the morning streets looked arid, dead, and she knew it wasn't just because it was early. For some reason, everything seemed a little less exciting without him here.

Stephen.

The thought of waking up and finding the days hollow for the rest of her life disturbed her. But what if...

Her mental fantasy machine kicked into gear. What would it be like to roll out of bed at *night* instead of in the morning? What would it be like to live for years and years, looking just as she did now, but with the gathered wisdom of maturity under her belt?

She leaned against her steering wheel, delving further into the what-ifs, toying with the idea of a life in darkness. She would dress for that nightlife, dress for the one thing that had made her feel alive for the first time in ages.

She would dress for Stephen.

In her mind's eye, she saw herself looking into a mirror, smoothing down a sleek red evening gown. Then Stephen would enter the picture, easing behind her to rest his hands on her bare shoulders. She could imagine the shiver that would travel her skin, imagine his smile as their gazes met in the looking glass.

His eyes would turn that blazing green, the color of arousal, as one hand skimmed over her collarbone. Gazes still connected, he would watch her closely while dipping his fingers into the bodice of her dress. As he traced her nipple to a peak, he would bend to her neck, fangs lightly scraping while he said, "You are the woman I have spent centuries searching for." It was a great fantasy. But she knew she'd never see him in a mirror.

Somewhere on the construction site, a horn beeped, and Kim started, grabbing her steering wheel, her dream so vivid that she had almost felt the pop of his fangs entering her skin. Her clit was stiff against her jeans, and she reached down to press against it, to assuage the erotic agony.

But it didn't work. No release, no relief.

Finally, she pushed away from the steering wheel. Why wasn't the fantasy enough?

Maybe, her common sense said, *biting and dry-humping your brains out night after night isn't what you really want.*

Kim flipped open her phone and cleared her head. As part of the League, it was her business to peer into the abyss; she just didn't want to do it with herself, because she couldn't stand to think of what might be looking back at her.

After donning an earpiece that would allow her to drive and chat at the same time, she accessed Troy's number using a voice command, then steered the Chevy onto the side road. Minutes later, as she pulled onto the freeway, her boss answered in a whisper.

"Kim?"

"Hey," she said, knowing he'd seen her caller ID. "How's Darlene?"

It sounded as if Troy was yawning. Then he said, "She's sleeping. It's lights out in her room."

Panic jabbed her. "You're not in there? Wait. I'm on my way—"

"No, no, Kim. I just stepped into the hall to talk to you, but I've stuck by her side like grade-school paste this whole time. Her parents are arriving at the airport soon to be with her." He sounded much more alert now. "How'd the rest of that date go?"

In the same way she couldn't bring herself to reveal Stephen to the League, she felt protective of what had happened with him and the rogue last night, too. But that was ridiculous, seeing as the bad vamp had attacked one of her own and she needed to tell the League what had gone down.

She decided to alter things to protect the preternatural, leaving out Stephen's vampire rescue efforts, of course. "Okay, don't go apeshit, but I went to the construction site last night."

"What?"

"Hi, apeshit? Not good to see you. Can I please talk to Troy again?"

"Kim, how many times have I told you—"

"I'm safe and sound, so dial it down, Troy. While we were poking around the site—"

"We?"

Kim rolled her eyes, then narrowly avoided an early-morning driver who almost cut her off. Dork. "Me and Stephen, and I don't need any comments about bringing him with me because you should be glad I had a wingman." She'd gone by the rules. Yeesh. "Anyway, while we were at the site, trying to avoid the cops, we encountered something that I think was our drainer vamp."

"Seriously? And?"

Damn. She couldn't explain how the rogue had uttered Stephen's name. What *could* she tell Troy without exposing her vampire guy?

"The creature was hiding its identity," she said, "so that's all there is to tell."

"Did it attack you?" Troy sounded dangerously pissed.

Kim tried not to be impressed by the alpha display. "We got away before it could do any damage." That was the truth, at least. Stephen had healed her and carted her off before she'd bled even a thimbleful.

"You're all right, though," Troy added. "I mean, you're not hurt or…"

"I'm fine. Stephen and I are just fine."

"Right. *Stephen.*"

By now, Kim had turned onto the 215. Even this early, there was a little traffic. "You got a problem with him?"

"Only that you should've left your overseas boy toy home last night, Kim. He's not League. *I* wouldn't bring a date on business. Besides, I—" Troy paused. "Forget it."

"What?"

"Nothing. I just get a bad feeling about the…guy. Your *date.*"

Besides asking him what he had against Stephen, she wanted to ask Troy when he'd last had a date, but she knew that he was somewhat of a workaholic even outside of the League. Still, every once in a while, Powder would mention Troy getting some, so she knew there was action going on in those pants of his.

"Let's move off of this subject." Kim didn't want him asking anything more about her vampire.

"Got it. Dropping Stephen."

His name lingered in the air, and Kim smiled, allowing it to saturate her once more. She conjured last night's exquisite mind game—a hypnotic fantasy joining them in a way she'd never thought possible. Regular men couldn't touch her vamp.

Just thinking about his history—a *highwayman,* by God—turned her on. He'd taken every romantic element and swathed her in it, binding her in the thrall of naughty wish fulfillment. He'd been the robber, she'd been the victim who'd had power. Delicious fantasy at its best.

A climax that had wracked her.

She blew out a hot-and-bothered breath.

"Kim?" Troy asked.

"Mmm?"

"Oh, man." She could almost see him shaking his head. "You think you can concentrate enough to hear something I noticed about Darlene?"

At the mention of her friend, Kim sat up straighter. "Go on."

"It's interesting—her bite wound is pretty much healed."

Absently, Kim reached up to touch the tattoo of last night's Stephen bite. There were no raised marks, anymore, and she'd make a bet that soon there'd be little evidence left of ever being bitten there. The rogue's bite on her other side was the same, thanks to Stephen's ministrations.

Kim pursed her lips. Boy, she was kind of a bite farm by now.

She geared up to ask Troy a question or two. "How did the police react to Dar's bite? And the doctors?"

"Well, one doctor joked about all the 'vampire attacks' they've seen coming through lately, and everyone laughed in that uncomfortable, shut-up-and-give-me-the-real-story way. All the authorities are going to be coming up with a million reasons why Darlene was attacked by something else, believe me."

That was good for Stephen and his family, Kim thought.

She blinked. Hell, when had her focus gone from the League's hunting to the welfare of vampires?

Something Stephen'd said came back to her.

If vampires are discovered by society at large, it would mean the end to our freedom.

Suddenly, that seemed more important than the more superficial excuse of showing the world these creatures existed and that she wasn't psychotic for thinking she'd been bitten.

When had she changed her mind?

She took her exit and signed off with Troy, not wanting to think anymore, just wanting to rest, to forget. "I think I'll call in sick to the bookstore today after I get enough shut-eye to function. Then I'll be at Dar's bedside."

"I'll take good care of her until then. And, remember, her parents will be here."

He was obviously playing hooky from his job today, too. See, he wasn't a hard-ass dictator, after all. Troy did have a heart.

"Thank you, boss man," Kim said.

They hung up and she headed home, knowing the route cold but trying to find her way, all the same.

HOURS LATER, opening his eyes from a deep sleep, Stephen intuitively felt the night falling outside the shelter of his family's cavern. He knew that, in the canyon, shadows would loom thick and summer-warm, knew that he would be leaving to take cover in their safety just as soon as he recovered fully from a day's slumber.

While he lay on his back and waited for his heightened vision to adjust from rest to reality, hints of Kimberly stamped the air.

Upon awakening last night, she had been the first thing he had seen, as well. For an unguarded moment, he had thought that he could get used to having her greet him in this manner all the time.

Now, he closed his eyes again, reconstructing the innocent, primal scent of her, conjuring the feel of her soft lips against his skin. A shudder sensitized his flesh, peaking him to near anguish in its rawness.

He was beginning to look forward to waking up since it was proving to be such a pleasure. Yet…

No, he should not be looking forward to anything at all. He had stopped anticipating and desiring back when Cassandra had taught him how dangerous that was. It was a lesson he would do well to remember now, especially since Kimberly had the potential to thwart his mission to find the rogue. All he had to do was consider what had happened last night, when he had been forced to choose between healing her and catching the other vampire.

But that was not what bothered Stephen the most. It was more about what had happened *after* the rogue had left and Stephen had taken Kimberly to that crumbling building…after he had indulged in a linked fantasy that had brought them both to shuddering climaxes. After biting her again.

It had been during Kimberly's afterglow, amid the ecstasy she had experienced from his hypnosis, that he had realized she was attached to the vampire. She craved the fantasy and nothing else.

Stephen fed on her blood, and she fed on this—a bite, something that brought her ecstasy and then wore off.

Any vampire could give her such a bite if they wished.

Beaten by the realization, he rose and went about his business.

That was all there could be for him—business.

After donning dark trousers and an equally black shirt that he left untucked, he bound his hair into its usual queue and strolled out of his sleeping crevice. In the common room, his brothers congregated near the Roman mural, discussing the contents of some papers spread before them.

"Look what the night dragged in," said Roger, his dark hair curled at his nape. Back in his human days, he had been quite the rake, on the run from an unhappy father who sought payback for the deflowering of his daughter. Fegan had found Roger very agreeable to disappearing and embarking upon a new life around the same time Stephen had done so.

Another vampire, Rupert, spoke from his lounging sprawl against the rock wall. A former pirate, he had been with Fegan longer than any of them, since his fellow crew members had emptied his pockets in New Providence and then left him for dead. From there, he had managed his way to England, keeping his dark beard and swagger intact, even after meeting Fegan and being recruited.

"Sam's been wanking on that Internet," Rupert said, "and he's found a thing or two."

Little Sam, who had been no more than a boy when he had joined the gang near the turn of the 19th century in New York, stuck a computer printout into the air. "Steve, this Van Helsing League is likely to be on to us soon. A girl named Kimberly Wight writes about a vampire who sounds an awful lot like you. Most of those entries aren't that recent but—"

"Rubbish," Roger said from his corner. "She never mentions a name, and I cannot even begin to tell you how many 'hot' vampires are about."

The younger vampire didn't lose steam. "I saw this column during my own research last night while Steve was out, and it *sounds* like him."

At Kimberly's apartment, Stephen had wiped out her current article, but it clearly had not affected the rest of her Internet site. It was time to master the newest technology if they were going to fight back in this day and age. And, here, Stephen had just ironed out his speech patterns to fit the era. Staying caught up was taxing.

"And," Sam added, motioning toward Henry, an original gang member who was currently plugged into an iPod, "this League has a radio show, too. Henry's listening to a podcast from a couple of nights ago about Kimberly Wight's most recent vampire sighting."

Roger seemed amused. Fegan had, no doubt, made a fool of Stephen and his second biting of this victim while Stephen was out of the shelter.

"This is the same woman, the 'accident'?" Roger asked. "*This* Kimberly?"

Stephen crossed his arms over his chest and grinned right back, though he didn't feel any lightness. "One and the same, though I am satisfied she will not be divulging any damaging details. Trust me on that."

"Oh, ho!" Roger slapped his thigh. "Listen to our Casanova. He can command with a heated whisper."

"Actually," Stephen said, raising a brow, "I can."

His brothers looked satisfied at that, clearly believing that Stephen had used his powers of mind control to stop Kimberly from revealing the gang. Little did they know that he had done no such thing.

He hadn't needed to.

Certainly, he didn't understand the reason she would be so adamant about hunting only to stay silent after finding him. It was something to monitor closely. Yet, it had occurred to him that, perhaps, her cooperation had something to do with wanting that bite she was always pursuing. Perhaps she thought that, by exposing him, he would no longer be available to please her.

If that were the case, then he was existing on borrowed time. How long would it be before she grew tired of this game?

A sense of horror engulfed him. In a short time, he had grown too intrigued by her. The night was far more interesting when she was wandering through it, far more filled with color and scent. He took more notice of that which had always been around him, and, without her there to bring out the details, he had forgotten...

"You're all not thinking straight." Little Sam assessed his brothers, his dark gaze dwelling on each one of them. He looked young, with his blond hair spiky and his eyes unlined by the coming of wrinkles, but he was the wisest of them all, really.

Roger looked unconcerned while Rupert gave a belly laugh, flinging away one of Sam's papers.

The youngest male vampire got to his feet and left the rest of the group, muttering, "They're getting too close is all I'm saying."

Stephen watched Little Sam's retreat, trying to read him, yet unable to do so.

As his gaze followed the other vampire out of the room, he noticed Fegan and Gisele newly arrived from their slumber crevices and doing their own watching from the other side of the cavern. There, Fegan leaned against a faded carousel horse stolen from a French prince's private amusement area; their creator had taken great pride and joy in privately torturing the park's guards, just for the fun of it. Gisele was sitting atop another one of the figures, a white steed, while still garbed in her pale, sheer nightdress.

Even from that distance, Fegan's low voice was clear.

"Looks like you've got more to worry about than just a rogue. I wonder if you need help out there."

"I have everything in hand." If Fegan were to send more gang members, Stephen would never hear the end of it. It would be a lacerating blow, just another swipe at the black sheep of the family.

And, though Stephen enjoyed the title, doing right by his brood really was everything.

At least, that is what he had always believed.

Gisele tussled Fegan's dark hair in a calming gesture. The creator glanced up at her, looking less devilish with her near to balance him.

"I'm not willing to hurt my children just because of your failings, Stephen," he said, "or to give up this life of ours. Maybe it's lost charm for *you,* but not everyone here feels the same."

Behind Stephen, footsteps signaled that at least a couple of his brother vampires had walked away. Without even turning, Stephen guessed them to be Roger and Rupert. Perhaps even Henry, as well. They had lost other brothers to hopelessness, and it was because Fegan just couldn't understand the monotony or the ensuing philosophical questioning.

Roger, especially, understood all of it too well since one of the fallen gang members had been a good friend. And, when Fegan had threatened that brother with a gruesome termination if they should ever cross paths again, both Roger and Stephen had lost that much more respect for their creator.

Fegan interrupted. "Are you becoming distracted out there, son?"

Stephen refrained from answering, yet his body shouted, almost betraying him.

Kimberly.

Gisele clutched the carousel steed's pole, her light brown eyes holding a hint of concern, or maybe there was fear there, as well. "Fegan, if he should fail—"

"Oh," their creator said, eyes gleaming, "if he should fail, we'll find ample opportunity to practice any surgical skills we've been dying to hone."

Unintimidated, Stephen turned his back and walked away. "Save your sadism." Bloody bastard. "Consider the rogue caught and think no more of it."

Their lack of confidence in his abilities angered him, hardened him. Nathan had not believed in him, either, and Stephen would not fail to provide this time. He was so blinded by frustration that he did not even stop to think if Fegan deserved his loyalties.

With that, he entered the dark tunnel leading to the world, his mind finally where it always should have been.

On his core mission.

"MY FRIEND already checked herself out?" Kim asked the receptionist at the hospital desk.

"That's what the records say." The Hispanic woman shrugged in sympathy. "She made a quick recovery. An amazing one, to tell you the truth."

It wasn't that Kim doubted *that*—with the help of the IVs and sleep, all of the draining victims had recovered. But Darlene had undergone Stephen's healing touch, so that, no doubt, had accelerated things.

No, the problem was that her friend hadn't bothered to call anyone to tell them she'd left the hospital, and that was strange.

Kim thanked the receptionist and opened her cell on the way to the exit. Troy answered on the second ring.

"Hey," she said, "did you know Darlene went home already?"

"We just found out." She could hear someone—probably Jeremy—futzing around with equipment in the background at headquarters. "She was still sleeping when I'd left in the late morning when her parents had come. I'd given them privacy but not before I'd put a crucifix around Dar's neck for some protection."

"So her parents probably took her home and she's sleeping it off there." It sounded reassuring, but a pit of worry sat heavily in her stomach. Maybe that was because she was ticked at herself for oversleeping, though. Kim had meant to be at the hospital much earlier, after taking just a catnap. But when her alarm hadn't gone off, her plans had been shot.

The sun had been setting by the time she'd gotten out of bed, and she still felt groggy. Not a big surprise, though, since last night had been kind of strenuous.

In many ways.

Blood surged, making her heart pound and reducing her to a rubber idiot. She leaned against a wall near the glass doors for support.

"Dar's probably too tired to be squawking on the phone right now," Kim added, hoping Troy would agree. "Maybe if I stopped by her place just to say hi…"

She only wanted to make sure Darlene was okay, that she wouldn't be another Lori.

On the other end of the line, Troy muttered to someone else and, before Kim knew it, Powder was talking, as hyper as usual.

"Kim? I tried to call Dar a few minutes ago, but her mom answered and said she wasn't up to having visitors. She's not even socializing with her own parents. She's knocked out, so I'd nix the house call until she gives the okay."

"But—"

"*But,* I know you're worried, and we are, too. We just want to have her back here, you know, spouting off her annoying stories about what happened at preschool today and all that. Speaking of which, when're you coming into headquarters?"

Hell, since she couldn't visit Darlene, maybe hanging out with the boys would provide some solace. From Troy's house, she could do some computer work, since she had no idea how to get hold of Stephen.

Wait. What if last night was the final time she'd see him? He hadn't made any promises to come back to her.

She felt as if she'd dropped something important and hadn't realized it was gone until she'd searched her purse for it. She backtracked, tracing over last night.

He'd left on a subdued note—not a good sign. What if he *was* gone for good?

"I'm on my way," she said, voice scratched.

As Powder said goodbye, she disconnected, stuffing her phone into her big bag, next to her hunting tools— items to repel a vampire.

But what if she didn't want to turn away a certain one? Or what if she'd done a good job of already doing it?

As she entered the deepening twilight and headed toward her car, she kept a hand on her crucifix. The rogue was also out here somewhere; no doubt, looking for another victim.

So when the air stirred, making the hairs on the back of her neck stand on end, she yanked the crucifix out of the bag, hoping she'd be repelling the right vampire.

11

KIM TURNED AROUND, brandishing the crucifix as a dusk-darkened breeze blew the hair from her face.

But all she saw was a streetlight blinking over a parking lot filled with cars.

Swallowing, she kept hold of the silver holy item and quickened her pace toward the Chevy. Maybe Darlene's health had improved, but that didn't mean Kim felt any better about what had happened to her friend.

As she jumped into her car and then locked herself inside, she realized that the last thing she wanted to do was go to League headquarters. What good would she do there? No, Kim knew exactly where she should be—Mystique, contacting the manager and trying to ask the early arriving employees questions about anything they might have seen.

And maybe Stephen would—

Nope. That wasn't why she was choosing to be out of headquarters and in a place where her vampire would have an easier time getting to her. Not at all.

Wasting no time, she started the car and donned her phone's headset, contacting Troy. As she aimed the Chevy toward the exit, she laid her intentions out to her boss.

When he decided that he and Powder would be coming with her, Kim had no problem with that. The boys would try to contact the manager on their drive over, then meet Kim at the inside club entrance.

Soon after disconnecting, she pulled into the Marrakech parking structure and alighted from her car, hand cupped over her bag-bound crucifix as she rushed toward the elevators.

But she never made it.

Someone stepped out from behind a pillar, arms crossed over his chest, his long coat lending him an imposing air.

Her heart seized, but her fear immediately turned into a bolt of yearning.

Stephen.

Cold to hot, her skin prickled, then seemed to melt. Her bones seemed to follow, all but pooling into themselves.

She was too overcome to move. Blood pounded, sending an inarticulate message to a brain that was no longer working quite right.

"Hi," she managed.

Stephen merely shook his head.

It took her a few moments to recover, so he took the opportunity to lecture her yet again.

"You seem to have learned nothing from last night's attack. If you were prudent, you would be inside your headquarters, not wandering the darkness."

"I've got…" She started to show him the crucifix, but realized that warding him off was the last thing she wanted to do. "Well, let's say I'm prepared. You had to know that I wouldn't give up this hunt."

"True, yet I didn't expect you to be tracking on your own." His gaze softened ever so slightly. "What are you doing here by yourself, Kimberly?"

Chug-a-chug, went her pulse. And it wasn't just because

he was in lusting range, either. She liked that he felt protective, even if she would never admit that out loud.

"You mean, what is a sweet little helpless human like me doing at the site of my friend's attack?" She'd switched to a mocking Southern-belle-accented voice. "Why ev-ah would I want to find the creature who hurt a loved one?"

"Kimberly…" he began.

"Hey, I wasn't about to go back to my place and wait for you to show up or not show up. I'm not going to wait around *period,* Stephen. Besides, I'm meeting Troy and Powder inside and we're going to sniff around as a group."

From the look on his face, she could tell that she'd hit the nail on the head. He *hadn't* been planning to include her in his search for the rogue tonight. She could understand his reasoning, too. After all, the other vampire had bitten her and Stephen hadn't been able to give chase. She didn't like knowing that her own ineptitude had kept the rogue free, but she wasn't planning to be caught off guard again.

"The last thing you need to do is worry about me," she said. "I mean it. I'll do my thing and you do yours."

Hold up. Shouldn't she be luring him into biting her right about now? Wasn't that how it was supposed to go?

Dumb question. Darlene's attack had changed everything. Still, someone needed to send her body that memo, because it was sure doing a good job of pursuing its own agenda. With every passing second, heat was rushing to her belly, sharpening to a point between her legs. She wanted to get closer to Stephen, to whisper for him to relieve the welcome anguish, to make her happy again.

Dammit, all she had to do was look at him—hell, *think* of him—and she went into a dither.

Just sidle a little closer, she told herself. *Put a hand against his chest and play with one of those shirt buttons to see what he might do next.*

The click of heels against concrete signaled a group's approach and effectively put an end to Kim's building fantasy. Three women dressed to impress passed by, spending a little too much time checking Stephen out. Kim sent them a back-off glare.

A slight smile quirked Stephen's lips, proof that he caught the look, then disappeared.

Misguided hope jerked inside of her, starting up a growl of heat through her veins.

"So," she said, "you gonna let me by and into the casino or what?"

Stephen held her gaze a moment too long. She thought she might've stopped breathing, too, because, seconds later, she sucked in a stream of air.

Why was she standing so far away from him again?

As if responding to her out-of-control pheromones, Stephen took his own step closer to her. "You know I can't let you near Mystique on your own, Kimberly. I would not be able to live with myself should the rogue get to you."

"I have another stake handy. And I pull a mean crucifix in a showdown."

"This is not a time to joke."

"That's not what I'm doing. Remember last night, how I almost got him?"

"Your stake inflicted a minor wound that has probably healed by now. He did far more damage to you."

At the reminder of the price they'd had to pay—letting the rogue go—Kim held her tongue. Maybe he was right— she shouldn't be here. But she wasn't a coward. She would rather end her life facing up to everything that dogged her than hide.

"Obviously," she said, "I'm on the right track if you're waiting for the rogue here, too."

He drilled a stare at her, eyes a brilliant green that hinted at an escalating craving. "Frankly, I would rather be at that construction site to see if our rogue returns, but I caught your scent."

The animalistic implication both scared her and thrilled her. He was attuned to her, just as much as she was to him. It was a basic link, a turn-on.

Her clit hardened, her sex dampening, swelling.

"So I'm on your vamp radar?" she asked in a strained whisper.

His gaze lit to a wilder green.

In spite of how much he tried to hide it, she had done what she had wanted to—become more than a passing thing for him. She mattered, lasting beyond what should've been a fleeting encounter. In her own way, she was a glint of eternity, an impression that he couldn't wipe away. Every word he didn't say just proved it.

Yet the victory didn't seem to matter as much as she thought it would. It was…flat. Why?

She must've had a freaky, needy look on her face, because his arms loosened away from his chest and his gaze fell to the ground.

Don't let him off the hook, she thought, not knowing why she wanted to push the issue, but having to, anyway. She knew she wanted hope, wanted to know what might've happened to Lori, but…there was something else. Something encoded within her that she couldn't solve.

"You caught my scent and you came to me," she said.

He seemed to be miffed by what he'd done—gone to her instead of where the rogue might show up.

Why wouldn't he admit that they'd become more to each other than an easy bite? Why couldn't *she* say it loud and clear?

Then, in a rough voice, he said, "If the rogue were to attack you again, I would blame myself. Do you realize what several lifetimes of guilt feel like? Can you imagine what it is to suffer until you decide to erase its presence in your conscience?"

Kim moved toward him, only wanting to make him feel better—make *herself* feel better. He went rigid, his arms returning to their defensive position over his chest.

"Why are you this way?" she asked. "What have you been through, Stephen?"

Something like a shadow passed through his gaze, a shard that sliced through color on its dark way. She held her breath, waiting for him to talk, because she was so sure he was about to—

A car's tires squealed, and he blinked. And there it was—he was back to being the closed-off mystery she had come to know. Or not know.

"Why can't you just tell me?" she asked as the car's noise faded. Her voice bounced off the empty, concrete spaces. "I'd do my best to understand, even though my life experience is nowhere near yours."

"Most of my history is irrelevant to what has transpired between us." He lowered his gaze on her, once again a little arrogant and a lot intimidating. "All you need to know is that I've been a criminal for centuries, not so much different from this rogue. That doesn't seem to be getting through to you. I have fed off of blood—robbed it, just as

I robbed travelers of their valuables. I'm not anything you should embrace."

She thought she heard a note of remorse in his tone. "Aren't you the vampire who's trying to stop the rogue before it can hurt more women? Tell me—where's the bad-boy awfulness of that?"

"I am only doing what I must to survive." He laughed sharply, gaze trained in the distance. "I am not so noble, at all. You just refuse to see the danger."

She thought of what he'd shared with her, mind to mind—bright moments from his mortal life, an exciting robbery scenario designed to fit her fantasies....

Yet there had always been an undercurrent of nefarious suggestion. She knew highwaymen had been criminals, but they had also been toasted in pubs and called *gentlemen.* Somewhere along the line, *someone* had romanticized them.

Just as she had romanticized The Bite.

But that didn't explain everything. She'd gone beyond fantasy and into a place of true danger with him—a place that frightened her because she couldn't figure it out. If she looked beyond the fantasy and deeper into Stephen—and into herself—that's where the danger really was.

Kim tried to steel herself, but she felt more like softened metal over a burning fire. "You want me to see the danger? I wish I didn't see so much, Stephen. Actually, I don't know if I want to see any more than I already do."

"Kimberly." He shook his head and relaxed his stance, his eyes losing their smolder. A look that could be defined as sympathy settled over his features. "I don't know what you're seeking, but you should not look to me for it."

Shouldn't look to him for it? He'd already made it pretty

clear that he couldn't provide those answers she'd sought about how Lori might be faring, but... There was something besides that. Something that had taken over once she'd learned that he didn't know much more than she, herself, did about the big picture.

She held back a wave of melancholy because it would chase away all the distracted passion that fueled her body. But she couldn't last against it. She wasn't that strong.

"You're the only thing that's made me feel alive in a long time," she said. "You bring back... I can't even explain it."

"You test the unknown with me."

"I... Yes."

A few aisles over, a group hooted and hollered on their way to the casino elevators. Stephen lowered his voice.

"Why do you look to me for fulfillment, then?"

She didn't want to talk about this, but then again, she really did. There'd been nobody else. Nobody who even came close to understanding.

"Last year, when Lori..." She exhaled. "Nothing made sense anymore. All the explanations for how the world worked—they didn't apply. It all seemed so senseless, like there wasn't any grand plan and that all of us had no reason for being here. I felt so...alone. Abandoned."

She paused, profoundly unsettled by the sentiment. It'd been the first time she'd admitted that.

Stephen didn't say a word, but she could see he was right with her. There was a flickering in his banked gaze, a glow of connection to what she was saying.

"Do you remember how it was with your brother?" she asked.

"I was already a vampire when Nathan left this world,"

Stephen said. "He was old enough so that his passing wasn't tragic, but I was new enough to feel the razor of his absence. His death was the first time I realized I would someday lose everything, that the world would march on after each life was extinguished."

Just as she had tried to march on.

Kim walked nearer, but it wasn't because she wanted to unbutton his shirt or to run her hands over his chest. No, she only wanted to be close. Just…close.

"What happened after you changed into a vampire, Stephen? Was there relief or…darkness? Are things different than they are during human life?"

He was already shaking his head. Sadness turned his gaze from green to a muddier shade.

Unreasonable anger flooded her. Her throat stung.

"Can you tell me?" she demanded.

She pushed at him, then balled her hands against his chest in apology. Tears, hot and unwelcome, prickled at her eyes, but she held them back.

He took her fists into his hands, closing his fingers around them. "I wish I knew, Kimberly, but vampires never touch the beyond. We stay and we linger."

She sank against him, closing her eyes.

Nothing would change. She'd always feel alone, wouldn't she? There'd always be abandonment.

Slowly, his arms enclosed her and he rested his cheek against the top of her head. The tears came, seeping into his shirt, but he didn't seem to mind. Not at all.

"I do think there is something more than this at some point," he added so softly she barely heard. "There has got to be something more."

She tried to believe him as she held tight to his coat and

gave in to the deep-seated misery that had driven her for more than a year.

Gradually, she realized that Stephen was holding on to her just as tightly.

AFTER CATCHING himself in such a weak moment, Stephen had pushed into a safer place, setting matters to rights and levelly suggesting that Kimberly meet her friends at Mystique while he kept an eye on her.

It was the only way he could do what he was meant to—continuing the search for the rogue and serving the family who sustained him.

Yet the diversion did not erase what had transpired between him and Kimberly. It burned like a crucifix held to a vampire's flesh, though he was not personally familiar with the sensation. Still, he felt scarred and marked on the inside, where he would feel pain all the more.

They went about their business with focused determination; him hanging back while Kimberly met her League friends to scour the nightclub and question the employees. He lurked in the shadows while combing the club for more clues, yet they all came up empty.

Nobody but Kimberly had even known he was there and, for a moment, he had felt just as hollow as those shadows, secure once again.

Then he had seen Kimberly wandering near the veiled club beds, and he knew without a doubt that his old existence wasn't enough anymore.

Afterward, she had bid her friends good-night and he'd escorted her back to the Chevy. At the same time, he cursed himself for not being able to let go of her long enough to set off in his own direction.

Yet, what could he do? In reality, if the rogue wished to be found, he would approach Stephen, himself, correct? That seemed the easiest way to contend with the criminal, although, Stephen was itching to do everything he could to find the other vampire first.

However, Stephen had the distinct feeling that the rogue was now working through the League just as surely as he had been, and it might be wise to keep the humans near. The attacks on both Kim and Darlene had been no coincidence.

Just as Kimberly was opening her car's door, she turned back to him, disappointment in the night's work obvious in her frown. "How about we go to the construction site?"

Stephen just stood in place. It was answer enough.

"Hey, I'm at the end of my rope here." She jammed her hands on her hips, red hair streaming over her shoulders and catching the stinging, pale garage lights. "We're getting nowhere."

"I'll be doing everything within my power to keep you away from that site." The horror of seeing the rogue digging into her neck with his fangs still lingered enough to serrate his words. "Don't test me on this. Mystique and this casino present somewhat of a challenge to an attacking vampire. That quiet site doesn't."

She narrowed her eyes at him, but when she found him to be resolute, she sighed. "Are you going to go there, at least?"

"I intend to."

"All right." She glanced at her watch. "If I can't go, too, I should get my butt home instead of to headquarters, where I'll be totally useless. I've got an early shift at work tomorrow and I can't be calling in sick again."

"I wonder if you and the team could, perhaps, refrain from any radio broadcasts, for now," he said mildly.

She sent him a tart smile. "You already know the answer."

But, when her smile fell and she glanced away, Stephen wondered if she was rethinking the League's indiscriminate activities. Was she realizing the damage they could do to him?

A light turned over in his chest, then darkened again. *Remove yourself,* he thought. *Survive.*

"I wish I could persuade you to stop them, luv," he said.

She raised her eyebrows at the light endearment. "Can't you hypnotize me into obeying your every command or something?"

He wasn't about to tell her that she was hard to mentally control unless she had invited him inside her head. It would give her more power over him than she already possessed.

"I respect your mental privacy," he said. "So off you go back home."

"Off I go." She hesitated, sending him such a cryptic glance that he could not even begin to decipher it.

But when he found himself reaching out to touch her hair, he became too caught up in her to think anymore.

The air seemed to go still as his fingers stroked the fine silk washing down her back. So soft, he thought, wishing he could bury his face against her, wishing the world would stay paralyzed so nothing else could interfere with the here, the now.

She hitched in a breath, then turned her face into his hand.

But then a car alarm went off nearby and the moment disappeared.

He backed away, mortified by his naked want of her. "Travel safe," he said.

She tried to say something, cleared her throat, then successfully communicated the second time. "You, too."

She smiled, more to herself than at him. Then, as that smile turned into a puzzled frown, she sat, closed the door, then strapped herself into the seat belt, revved the engine and departed with a casual wave.

Careful to note if anyone was watching—and they weren't—he took off after her, a blur that would only be seen by another vampire.

But he didn't sense any other presence, so he followed her to the unremarkable apartment complex she called home. After he made certain she was safe, he would visit the construction site.

But only after.

He met her in the parking lot and, when she invited him into the lobby so he could see her directly to her door, he told himself he needed to make certain the rogue was not trailing her.

Really, though, Stephen knew that he just wished to stay with her, to satisfy the never-ending hunger that gnawed the lining of his belly.

A bite, he thought, needing it badly. Not for the blood, but because it was all he could give this woman who made him feel so deceptively alive.

They rode the elevator to her floor. A short trip, but uncomfortable nonetheless for a vampire who was aching for a taste.

He was blind to everything but Kimberly as the doors opened to the upper lobby. That is, until they passed the stairwell and two elderly people opened the metal door to enter.

The man, who had silver, bristly hair and a stout disposition, held out his arms to Kimberly. His companion, a vibrant woman with a bob and a beaming smile, patted

Kimberly on the shoulder as she came to hug the man. She was matronly and genuine.

"Well, well, Miss Kim," the older man said in an exaggerated late-night whisper.

An East Coast accent and a hint of alcohol laced the air as Kimberly then hugged the woman with great enthusiasm.

The couple had been drinking wine. An expensive burgundy, Stephen thought.

They kept their voices low as they completed their greetings. All too soon, the attention was on Stephen. Yet he knew how to react—humanly.

"Who have we here?" the woman said.

"Oh." Kimberly seemed caught off guard. "Stephen. He's…well, you know, up here for…fixing my computer."

The older woman's gaze lit up. "Good to meet you, Stephen!" She pumped his hand in greeting.

The old man merely took stock of Kimberly's obvious "date." The scrutiny made Stephen shuffle, then recover. Odd.

Kimberly motioned to the couple. "This is Mr. and Mrs. Cornish, two people who refuse to take elevators when there're stairs."

"You've got that right," Mr. Cornish said, laughing. "No sense in wasting electricity when I can work off my meals."

As a greeting, Stephen bowed his head in respect, mindful that, even though the couple seemed older than he, Stephen was actually far beyond their years. Still, respect was in order.

"A pleasure," he said.

Kimberly seemed very eager to turn the focus away from him.

"Where were you two night owls this time?"

Mr. Cornish spent another eternal second gauging Stephen before he smiled, then put a loving arm around his wife. Stephen actually exhaled at the reprieve.

"It was off to that new restaurant, Umberto's, near Red Rock Station. Fantastic lasagna Bolognese, Kimberly. They have a late-night jazz show, too."

While he chatted, his wife watched him with such affection that Stephen almost felt as if he could not comprehend the existence of it. Emotion ran deep between these two, culled from years of happy living, no doubt.

Two words raced through him—soul mates.

Yearning bubbled, but it was not the type that forced his teeth to lengthen or heated his body.

This was something uncommon and foreign. A vague desire to experience their type of link—one that didn't require reaching into a prey's mind.

He wondered if he could capture its taste with a bite, if he could just…

He forced his mind to go black. Unacceptable. He survived on blood and didn't need to bite for any other reason. Certainly, a vampire such as Fegan would disagree—the creator would have attacked the Cornishes merely because he could—but Stephen had developed boundaries over the years. He was no angel, but couldn't he strive to be less of a devil?

Besides, true, shared affection was one thing he could never have, not even with a bite. If anyone knew that, it was Stephen.

Then he felt Kimberly's gaze upon him, and he found himself turning to her, discovering the only person who could make him believe differently.

12

WHEN STEPHEN FINALLY locked gazes with her, Kim felt as if a wind had blown out the windows of her sheltered defenses and rushed straight through her.

In his eyes, she could see it—he wasn't as far from humanity as a vampire probably should be. Standing here with the most loving couple on Earth was having the same effect as it usually had on her—the Cornishes made it seem that something more existed for everyone.

They reminded her of the old Kim—the girl who'd had *someone* and, therefore, some*thing* in her life besides continual restlessness.

Stephen must've realized that he'd let down his barriers, because he straightened his posture, and his gaze seemed to cool. He turned back to the still-chatting Cornishes and donned a polite smile while hearing their opinion about the restaurant.

Kim wanted to push him, to prod him, to do anything to get another genuine reaction out of him. For a brilliant second, she had seen something that was like a crack in the sky—a glimpse into the world she'd been looking for, a definition of what had been missing from their last intimate encounter.

She held her breath, waiting for him to offer another hint

of that Stephen, the one she wanted to save more than any fantasy or bite.

But he just kept nodding his head as Caroline Cornish raved about Umberto's wine list.

Then Kim heard Mr. Cornish's voice filtering through, and she knew that he was addressing her. Her eyes had trouble focusing on the older man.

"Excellent place to have a romantic dinner, Kim," he finished. "You and Stephen need to go there sometime."

She noticed that the elderly couple was giving Stephen one of those "meaningful looks" that meant they were trying to see just how serious he was about Kim, especially since he was going into her apartment at this time of night.

"We'll check it out," she said. "Umberto's, that's the name?"

Mr. Cornish nodded suspiciously, but his wife gave an "Aaaahhh," as she bought Kim's attempt to make Stephen's presence harmless.

"I guess you computer nerds make pretty late house calls," the mister said to Stephen just before Mrs. Cornish nudged him with an elbow.

At her urging, the older couple proceeded into the hallway, and Kim glanced at her vampire "date," who seemed untouched by the entire encounter.

And here she was thinking that the earth had moved under their feet during that one long, jarring glance. Wow, great to see that any epiphany had totally passed *him* by.

Kim rolled her eyes. So…okay. She had gotten emotional about a vampire. It wasn't enough that she had been obsessing over a bite, but she had to go and supplement that with actual feelings. Good move.

When they reached their respective doors, they all paused to say good-night.

Mr. Cornish sent Stephen a stern look as his wife entered their place without him. "I hear these computers don't take too long to fix nowadays."

He tapped his watch, only to be dragged inside by Mrs. Cornish. She popped out her head and waved a final farewell.

"Don't mind him, Kim. You have a nice night."

"You, too, Mrs. Cornish."

When the lady waved one last time and then shut the door, Kim felt herself blushing. Good God, she couldn't even look at Stephen because of Mr. Cornish's shotgun-dad act.

"He misinterprets things sometimes," she said, unlocking her door and going inside.

"Who, that nice little man?" Stephen shut her door behind him. "And here I believed you truly did need help with your computer. I was set to poke around in it."

Her face heated up even more, spreading a flush throughout her body. Had that been some sort of tech-based innuendo? And why would it have made her all flustered?

"You poked around enough the other night when you erased my Web column," she said, pretending she hadn't gotten the joke—if he'd indeed been flirting in that dry British vampire way of his. She struggled to regain her composure by pointing to a black futon draped with Mexican blankets. "Why don't you sit while I get us something to drink."

But he just stood there. Finally, she brought herself to look at him, even though it was the hardest thing she'd done since… Well, maybe ever.

He was watching her intensely, yet, when she met his gaze, he assumed his usual negligent stance.

What were you just thinking? she wanted to ask. *What's going on?*

But, after a loaded second, he grinned like a lady-killer and sat on the couch, finally obeying her command with amused grace.

She was on the cusp of blurting out everything that was going unsaid between them. Damn, she wanted to get it all into the open. But why? What would be the use? He was a *vampire,* and she'd studied up on them enough to know that there was no future here. Not unless he made whatever big sacrifice it took to be human again—if what she'd seen in his mind about how he missed those days was true and he wanted to go back to them.

Or maybe *she* could…

Kim swallowed, recalling her morning fantasy—the red dress she would wear for Stephen during one of their many nights together, the continual bites… Dumb. That had only been a daydream, an idle thought.

Hadn't it?

Unwilling to even consider the ramifications of becoming one of the undead, she went into her small kitchen, busying herself by putting on a pot of water for tea.

"What's your poison?" she asked, almost laughing at herself. Her. Kimberly Wight. A bloodsucker. She'd reached the edge of sanity.

"Besides the usual? I'll have whatever you're having."

Kim paused while fetching a box of random tea bags from her cupboard. "Vampires are allowed to drink more than blood?"

"Yes, we're allowed. But anything else doesn't provide much enjoyment, so most of us don't bother." He watched her grab mugs from the cupboard, then shut it. "Alcohol doesn't settle well."

"I'm sure your addictions run more to the exotic, anyway."

STEPHEN RAISED a brow at the comment. Addictions weren't always exotic.

He shifted in his seat as Kimberly tucked a strand of red hair behind an ear. Sometimes addictions were based on a craving for the normal, for the one-in-a-million thing that brought a missing serenity to light.

As she moved around the kitchen, he appreciated every nuance—the way she determinedly cleaned up after herself as she put their tea together, the way she put a finger to her lips as she decided what to place on the tray.

It was easy to deceive himself into thinking that he was mortal right now, that he was waiting for Kimberly to sit with him and sip from her mug while they talked about their days at work. That they were so very happy—as happy as Kimberly's neighbors—to see each other now that night had fallen.

But he had a rogue vampire to catch, and there was nothing remotely human about what would come afterward when Fegan got his greedy hands on the deviant.

Kimberly was walking toward him with the tray, two steaming mugs among the earthenware sugar and honey pots. When she leaned over to give him a mug decorated with a skimpily garbed superheroine who held a whip, he caught the scent of his favorite prey above the orange spice of the tea.

Desire shot up through his chest like a hanging tree that had done all its growing in one thrust. Branch tips tore at him on their way up.

He contained himself, holding the warm mug while Kimberly sat in a lounging chair opposite him.

She cupped her mug awkwardly, looking just as ill at ease as he felt. Where had the siren gone? Who was this quiet woman?

And why did he want her as much as the other?

"I've been wondering about something." She laughed a bit, telegraphing embarrassment.

"You've never hesitated in asking before." Absently, he leaned forward, resting his forearms on his thighs and cradling the mug with both hands. He tried to fill his senses with the tea instead of her, but it was a losing battle.

"Okay…" She ran a hand over the side of her leg, as if wiping moisture off and onto her jeans. "You… Well, a few nights ago you said you didn't bite women more than once, and you only made a mistake with me because there've been so many bites that you'd forgotten."

This wasn't a subject he wished to dwell on.

She kept her hand on her thigh, fingers curved. "But you've bitten me three times now. Why? I mean, before everything ends with the rogue and you go your way and I go mine, maybe you could just tell me."

For some reason, her Southern accent was really coming out now, perhaps because she was forcing herself to be casual, even flippant. Usually, her words were less affected, just as he had trained his own to be over the years.

"I suppose my appetite has increased in this desert air," he said in an attempt to seem removed.

Kimberly hesitated and, in that moment, he could see the stain of rejection on her lovely face.

In spite of himself, he rushed to make her feel better, his voice lowering to a near tremble that he didn't recognize at all.

"Your spirit touches me, Kimberly. Is that not enough reason?"

She raised her pale eyes to his, and lightning struck.

It illuminated all that he had kept back inside—the forgotten emotions, the maddening desire to hold someone dear, the pain of being unable to do so.

He wanted her to know, wanted to see how she would react to a vampire who had crossed the line and done the unthinkable—become enamored of his prey.

"Before now," he said, words rushing, "I have been mired in a place that has kept me sane. A place where I have not been forced to feel. I was there when I first bit you. Yet you were there, too, weren't you? Your sister had only just passed on, and when I took my fill of your blood, there was nothing to move me. Nothing but the same static I endured night after night."

"But then your bite changed me." Her eyes were so wide, so afraid. "I guess I became the one woman who wouldn't take no for an answer from you, and you couldn't help but notice me again...and again."

"No, you didn't force me to bite you more than twice, Kimberly. Unlike the first time, you have grown in strength, and you are the only bite who has ever been able to control *me*." There. He had said it. "Not the other way around."

"I...control you?"

She touched her chest with such stunned delicacy that he almost dropped his mug.

He set it on an end table before he mortified himself.

She cleared her throat. "I guess that's something you shouldn't have let out of the bag, huh, Stephen? I can go around making you my hot servant now."

Though she was teasing, his hackles rose, and he spoke before thinking. "I am *no* woman's servant."

Before he could mark the hurt reaction he expected—a sight that would be his undoing—he stood, then walked out of her range. Her scent...her body heat... It was all starting to overwhelm him.

"Stephen."

He stopped, slowly realizing that she had commanded him. But it was not because of a mind trick, he was certain of that. It was because she just *had* that power over him, and there was nothing preternatural about it.

"I've asked you before," she said, "and you never answered. What happened to make you so..."

"Difficult?" he supplied, the word vitriolic.

Silence beat through the room.

Why shouldn't he give her an answer? Maybe it would convince him of this folly in being with her if he heard himself say Cassandra's name, if he relived an anguish that had escaped him for more than a hundred years.

"There was a woman, of course," he said, coming to stand in front of a framed picture of another superheroine. The glossy surface didn't reflect him, but in its clarity, he could imagine Cassandra's face. "She provided a lesson in never hanging on to anything… anyone."

"Just like the lesson you learned about your brother? Did this Cassandra turn her back on you like Nathan did?"

"No, it wasn't quite like losing the love a family." Seeing Cassandra—a woman for whom he had lived passionately—staring in utter dread at the sight of him wasn't nearly the same. "My love for her was a different one. It was…all-consuming. It ruled me."

When he risked a look at Kimberly, she was clasping her arms in front of her chest, as if enclosing herself.

"I would watch her in the upstairs window," he continued softly, "her blond hair shining as she brushed it in front of her mirror. During each visit, I would draw an inch closer, closer, telling myself her performance was only for me. Then I would whisper, planting the thought in her mind that I meant no harm. Soon, she came to the window, where I romanced her. Yet there was never a bite, not even after she invited me into her room."

"Did you two…" Kimberly didn't finish.

"I made love without any sort of penetration, if you wish for the details."

"It's not that I *want* to hear them, Stephen."

Her jealousy was all but palpable and, for some reason, that made him feel important, so very required.

A tremble skated over his limbs, burrowing under his flesh and to his belly. "I became too excited one night, and everything I had been holding back emerged—the monster. The ugly truth of what I am."

"And she screamed," Kimberly said, as if privy to Stephen's vision. And perhaps she was by now. "She screamed until her family broke down the door. But you were already gone."

"Gone," he repeated. "Yet I returned to her window again and again, hidden, knowing I could never have her. As I watched, the anger grew until I could feel it no more. Every night made me into a walking, used-up vessel."

Bit by bit, the past faded from his gaze, revealing Kimberly, her jaw tight as she shook her head.

"You don't agree?" he asked.

"You're not half as bad as you think, Stephen. You believe you're this brooding terror who can't relate, yet here we are—the vessel and the victim who *didn't* scream when you turned your so-called worst on me."

All too true—she wanted the vampire in him. It was that simple—and that terribly wrong.

"Yup, here we are," she repeated, almost as an afterthought. She swallowed hard, and her voice cracked when she added, "Here *I* am."

Everything plastered into a timeless second. Even his heart stopped beating.

A choice. She was offering him some sort of choice, but he wasn't certain what it was. Truthfully, he didn't want to know, and that was keeping him from pursuing its meaning.

Say something, he thought. *Tell her what you have been keeping back. Tell her that you are so bewildered by what is happening that you—*

Kimberly's phone rang, and she jumped.

Please answer it. Please.

It rang again, but she only stared at him, as if thinking his response was imminent.

Finally, he could stand it no longer. Out of pure desperation, he went to her carrying bag on the kitchen table and flipped open the phone himself.

"Hello?"

"Uh, hello?" said the male voice at the other end of the line.

It sounded like one of Kimberly's League people, thank goodness.

"Let me give you to Kimberly," Stephen said, walking to her and handing her the cell.

Their fingers brushed, and he tried to get away as fast as he could, but she grabbed his wrist.

The male's voice kept saying "Kim? Kim? Kim?", punching the atmosphere where the thud of heartbeats should have been sounding instead.

But Stephen *didn't* have the heart for this.

Breaking away, he left her to take the phone, her expression falling.

Enraged more with himself than anything else, he headed toward the door.

"Wait, Stephen," she told him, hand covering the mouthpiece. She spoke into the phone. "Powder, Darlene's *there* and she's talking about the attack?"

Suddenly, Stephen was not about to go anywhere.

ON THE DRIVE OVER, Kim had been so spurred by Powder's phone call that she barely had time to be uncomfortable around Stephen.

True, there were about a hundred-thousand reasons to be fidgety, and 99.9% had to do with offering up herself to him and then being rejected.

Luckily for her ego, she'd been so busy replaying Powder's phone call on the short ride to headquarters that both of them had a reprieve. And she could tell Stephen was grateful for it, because he was in typical male-avoidance mode—all manly quiet and relatively relaxed as they sped along in her Chevy.

Vampires. Not so different from human guys, after all.

"That's all Powder kept telling me," Kim was saying as she pulled into the subdivision where Troy's house was located, one sand-colored dwelling after the other flying by. Most of them seemed to be empty lately because residents normally fled the summer desert heat for cooler vacation spots. "He kept saying that Darlene was asking for me and I should get over here."

"I'm curious to see how she fares." Stephen was in his corner, gaze trained out the windshield. "I appreciate your allowing me to come along to assess her."

"Assess. How formal."

He laughed quietly, knowing a potshot when he heard one.

Hell, he deserved a poke or two. So did she, because they were both acting as if neither of them had gushed their hearts out back at the apartment.

As she pulled into Troy's driveway, she continued to do her best to pretend what had happened hadn't happened, even though she knew damned well it *had* happened. Talk about confusing.

She'd impulsively tested the waters, and Stephen had spit her back out.

Or had he? He'd been reluctant to reveal his own thoughts, and she'd taken that for a negative. Was she right?

Sure she was. A girl with as much experience as her knew how to read a male pretty well, vampire or not. His desire to have a hole split the ground and swallow him up had been about as obvious as a real crater in her apartment floor would've been.

After shutting off the car and getting out, she invited him into the house, but he refused, citing the many crucifixes that Troy had recently positioned by the entrance. Instead, Stephen asked Kim to somehow bring Darlene outside so he could scan her.

Cut bait and run—that's what he was doing. She knew the drill for setting yourself up for an easy escape when she saw it.

After she left Stephen to do his thing outside, she entered the house and saw Powder pacing in the family room, where the TV was off. That was weird, but it was even stranger to see the look on his face—absolute befuddlement.

Then she heard the laughter from a guest room, where Darlene usually worked on the computer.

"Sounds like a pickup bar back there," Kim said.

Powder shrugged.

They both headed toward the sound, and Kim halted at the bedroom's threshold.

There, on the bed, sat Darlene, her dark corkscrew hair loose and wild, her skin glowing with the aid of sexy, smoky makeup. She was dressed in a way that made Kim's eyes about bug out of her head—a black top that showcased her ample breasts, tight matching pants and screw-me heels. Jeremy and Troy were gathered around her, leaning forward in telling body language—some kind of dialect brain-dead guys with hard-ons would speak.

Then she ran another gaze over Darlene, realizing what was happening.

The Bite, she thought, knowing what it'd done to her a year ago and seeing it being played out again in her friend.

Had it been the same for the other draining victims, too?

Darlene spotted Kim, and everyone turned to see her still standing in the doorway like yesterday's news.

"Well, come on in, Kimmy," Darlene said, kicking one heel up and over her knee as she leaned back on the mattress. "I don't bite."

Troy and Jeremy cracked up, and Kim shot them a harsh glance.

Then they shut their traps.

Kim hesitated, not liking how she was reacting. Shouldn't she be ecstatic to see her friend up and about? So why was there a persistent unease holding her back from joining the good times?

"How're you feeling?" she asked Darlene instead.

Her friend pulled an isn't-it-obvious face. "Lots better. A whole lot."

At the same time, Troy and Jeremy both said, "Better, yup, better." Behind Kim, Powder made a *hmmph* sound.

"Say, you two." Kim nodded to the woody twins. "Can I talk with my friend for a sec?"

"Well…" Jeremy said.

Troy looked at Kim, really looked, then seemed to come to a semblance of the sense he used to have. "Right." He shook his head slightly and stood. "Kim hasn't caught up with Darlene yet, and we've got work, anyway, Jer."

He actually seemed embarrassed.

As he passed Kim, she pursed her lips. It wasn't that she was jealous of his attentions toward the newly sexed-up Darlene…

Okay. It kind of was, but only because her idiot ego had so recently been tweaked by Stephen.

She thought of the vampire waiting outside, and a blast of wet heat filled her.

Damn libido. Didn't it know when to stop?

The boys cleared the room, and Kim shut the door behind them, but not before issuing a warning that she'd kick their cabooses if anyone eavesdropped.

Then, after the closed door put an exclamation point on her comment, she smiled at Darlene and approached. "You don't know how glad I am to see you. Your mom said you didn't want visitors—"

"You can't stand it, can you?"

Kim halted, doing a double take. "What?"

Darlene rose from the bed and went to the computer, giving Kim what amounted to a cold shoulder. "You hate that you're not the queen of them anymore."

Kim couldn't believe this—mainly because Darlene was right. She'd thrived on what The Bite had done to her, but now, after these last couple of nights with Stephen, the novelty had worn off and become a baffling reality.

"Dar—"

"You hate that you're not the only special vamp girl now."

There was nothing she could say to make her friend think any differently, not at this point. Kim remembered being bowled over by her new confidence, too, and nothing would've gotten through to her in those first few weeks. Or maybe ever.

Nothing except meeting her vampire again.

The click of Darlene's fingers on the keyboard was like tiny bops to Kim's head.

"The guys tell me you haven't been around much

lately," Darlene said, still facing the computer. She was checking e-mail. "So I took the liberty of writing a column to replace yours tonight. It's about *my* encounter this time."

"*Your*…" Kim just about chomped on her tongue. *Jealous.* She wasn't going to be that way because she had something much better than a bite itself waiting outside.

Then again, maybe she didn't have Stephen at all.

Darlene's fingers had gone still. "Whoa."

"Whoa, what?"

"Whoa, I… Read this e-mail."

Kim scanned it, then blinked and read it again.

Your blood-draining vampire hangs around the abandoned E-Z-Duz-It gas station near Sloan, NV. Check that castoff semitrailer at the back of the main building.

"Whoa," Kim repeated, already halfway to the door. "Dar, do me a favor? Explain this to the boys?"

"Where're you— Wait for me outside, okay? Let me go to the…bathroom, and I'll be right there. Just wait outside."

Kim barely registered Darlene's request as she stumbled out of the room and into the hall. Everyone around the area knew where the old EZ was—just off the 15 on the way to the state line.

Wait until she told Stephen. Maybe the rogue wouldn't be at the station right now, but, with Stephen's powers, they might be able to get a fix on the baddie's identity from clues.

She jammed through the front door, Darlene still yelling at her to wait outside and she'd be right there, too. The boys, who were waiting in the family room, didn't even have time to interfere with Kim's frantic dash.

"Stephen?" she called, running down the entry walk to

her car, then opening her door with the intention of grabbing her fight bag. "I've got something! Stephen!"

With a whoosh of air, he was there, standing before her.

For a drawn-out moment, she saw it in his eyes—he'd been thinking about what had happened back at her apartment. But urgency forced her to put that aside.

For now.

She told him what the message said. "So let's go. You can fly us there—"

He was shaking his head.

"But—"

"Promise me that you'll stay inside this house," he said, his voice so even that it made her want to scream. "The crucifixes make it safe, and I'll contact you when it's over."

She'd seen too much, learned too much, to believe vampire hunting was anything less than serious. Common sense told her that his request to stay was logical, and that she should swallow her pride and just do it.

She tried to maintain her dignity even while a lump lodged in her throat. "You don't want me around to thwart another chance at capturing the rogue, huh?"

The moonlight revealed his bittersweet expression. "I respect you, Kimberly. Your passion and courage. And if I thought it would not be my downfall, I would have you by my side."

Why did it sound as if he wasn't just talking about the rogue chase?

With something like regret, he reached out to cup her jaw, running a thumb over her cheek until she almost fused against him. Dizzy, so dizzy when he touched her.

"I'm coming back," he said raggedly. "Believe that."

Then, as quickly as he'd appeared in her life, he took

off out of it, leaving nothing but an almost imperceptible quiver of air in his wake.

But she didn't have time to feel anything at his departure because Darlene came tearing out of the house, followed by the League members. Troy was stuffing an assortment of vampire weapons—holy water, ear plugs for any attempted hypnosis, a crucifix—into his jeans pockets.

At Kim's curious glance, he raised his eyebrows, then shot a loaded look to the sky where Stephen had already disappeared.

In that moment, Kim realized that Troy knew more about Stephen than he'd said out loud.

"Shut up already," Darlene was yelling over her shoulder as she hustled to Kim's car.

Powder was on her tail. "I'd just like to know who you could be on the phone with, telling them that Kim's outside."

Oh, God.

Just as Kim got the first twitch of something being very, very wrong, a force like a two-by-four slammed into her, dragging her through the air and into the open desert at the back of Troy's house.

The next thing she knew, she was skidding on the sand, the ground abrading one arm as a bunch of scrub loomed in the moonlight. An old rickety shack, tarps flapping at its sides, leaned on the horizon. It was surreal in her scrambled vision.

She coughed, getting to her hands and knees, reaching for her weapons bag.

And finding that it wasn't with her.

In the background, she heard the League screaming

and running toward her, and she opened her mouth to tell them to get inside the house.

But a shadow covered the moon, cramming her words right back into her throat.

The shape's coat flapped in the wind and, for a second, Kim thought it might be Stephen.

It wasn't.

And when Darlene ran laughing and panting into the shape's arms, Kim realized that her friend belonged to this vampire just as surely as she, herself, belonged to her own.

13

As Darlene flung herself into the rogue vampire's arms, the League members slid to their own graveled halts.

All except Troy, who managed to skid right next to Kim on the ground. Then he dug into one of his pockets and lifted something to his ears, but she was too preoccupied to think any more of it.

"Did I do it right?" Darlene was asking her vampire. "I got Kim outside, and Stephen took off for the EZ, just like you wanted."

The rogue's voice was deep and smooth, touched by a British accent like Stephen's. "Your friend will provide wonderful leverage, dear, and Stephen is certainly going to be listening to what I have to say at this meeting, now that I'll have better control of the situation. Thank you for your help."

Hazily, Darlene hugged her vampire while sparing a sorry glance to Kim. "He said Stephen would come back for you, that he'll do anything for you, and that's why you're here, Kim. I had to do it for him. I *wanted* to. You understand, don't you?"

Understand being whipped by a vampire and finding yourself doing things you normally wouldn't for another bite? Um…yeah. Kim understood completely, but she still couldn't believe Darlene had betrayed her.

The rogue gently guided his love slave behind him while stepping forward, taking off his sunglasses and pulling back the hood from his jacket, which he was wearing under his coat. Moonlight revealed longish brown hair that waved near high cheekbones, full lips and wide, almond-shaped eyes that glowed a burning amber.

Behind Kim, Powder and Jeremy sucked in a breath, maybe because the rogue looked like Johnny Depp. Or maybe he was just that vampire-gorgeous.

Adrenaline skewed her perception. One arm felt pulped from scraping the ground, but she really didn't care.

The vampire casually pointed to all of them in turn. "Don't move—and stay silent."

She didn't know how his voice affected the others, but she found she couldn't budge, even though her brain was screaming for her to start, dammit, *start.*

Mind control? How was it that Stephen couldn't hold her in sway while this vamp had no problem?

Troy, who was so close that his arm brushed hers— *ouch*—eased back an inch. *He* was capable of moving.

The rogue continued coming forward, halting about ten feet away from them. Even though Kim couldn't command her body, her veins began to tremble. Time seemed to press in on itself, flipping inside out.

Stephen. How could she warn him like this?

"I'm afraid Darlene was not supposed to bring her League anywhere near this…gathering," the rogue said. "Most of you aren't a part of what is between me and the other vampires. Except for you," he said to Kim. "You're quite valuable to my cause. Stephen *will* listen this time, now that I know how to persuade him."

Kim got a bad feeling about this. In fact, she suspected she might find herself the rogue's hostage once again.

Behind the vampire, Darlene called out, "I'm sorry. They ran out behind me, Edward—"

Edward.

"—and after I pulled up that e-mail, all I wanted to do was see you again. I didn't have time to tell them why they needed to stay inside. It's been too long since…"

"Since last night, when you were bitten. Yes, Darlene, I know, dear."

His voice was like clotted cream dripping down Kim's skin. It should've sent her into convulsions of lust, this warm bath of sensation, but she stayed cold. Even the shakes consuming her had been jarred by fear instead of desire.

Stephen—what did this rogue have planned for *Stephen?*

She had to stop this creature.

The slightest movement at the edge of her vision made Kim pause. While Darlene was holding the vampire's attention, Troy had subtly reached into a pocket again. Meanwhile, the League's traitor sounded hopeless in the background.

"I did everything you wanted me to without ever asking why."

"As I'd hoped you would," Edward said, still watching Kim, glowing eyes narrowing in the near dark. He ignored Darlene and talked to his new prey, instead. "So now I have time to appreciate the details of you. Stephen's mortal woman. I never thought I'd see the day again. Not after Cassandra."

At the sound of Stephen's name, Kim's skin flared in awareness. Regrets were permeating her now that she might not have a chance to say *anything* ever again. She wanted to tell him that he was more than just a bite, so much more.

But where was he?

Above her, Edward sighed, clasping his hands behind his back. He had a noble bearing, probably a remnant of his extensive past. She wondered how he knew Stephen, but she couldn't find the energy to break this hold and talk.

Next to her, she sensed more movement. Troy. Was he using her arm as a shield while he kept inching toward a weapon in his pocket?

Why the hell could he do that when she…

The earplugs, she thought. He'd used his earplugs against the vampire's voice commands.

Edward lifted his face to the night, as if searching. Then, finding nothing but the moon and stars, he frowned. In the meantime, Darlene had approached again, sliding a hand up his arm as she fixed a worshipful look on him.

"Maybe," she said, "while we're waiting, you could… you know."

"No, not now." Edward smiled at her. "I'll reward you with another bite later, just before I…" He smile grew as he cut himself off. "Just be patient, all right, *muffin?*"

He sounded as if he were getting sick of the high-maintenance groupie thing.

As Kim watched her friend—her changed, bite-starved friend—back off Edward the vampire, shame invaded her. Darlene had obviously become a Renfield, a servant who'd do anything to please the master. If Kim had to guess, she would say that, unlike the other draining victims, Darlene was under deep hypnosis and had been ever since her bite.

Kim's lungs seemed to go shallow without much air to expand them. Had *she* been Stephen's servant for the last year?

No, even Stephen had said that she had power over *him.*

She wasn't like Darlene. She knew it. Yet Edward obviously hadn't drained Kim's friend as he had the others; he'd taken her mind more than her blood, and Kim knew without being told that he'd only done it because Darlene was useful. He'd gone the back route into cornering them all.

While Darlene slunk off to sit near a small hill, her gaze on Edward all the while, the vampire himself grew restless.

"We shan't have long to wait," he said to Kim. "Stephen will be here because *you* are. Yet it seems to me that having fewer of you uninvited lot around would be all the better. So…"

Keeping one hand behind his back, he flicked the other wrist, motioning and saying, "Sleep." A heavy thud told Kim that Jeremy had gone down like a sack of garlic. The rogue aimed again, producing a lighter crash that no doubt came from Powder.

Kim braced herself for her turn…

But that was when Troy went for it, standing and raising his hand in what felt like slow motion while the vampire moved in real time.

Just as Powder hit the ground, Edward gracefully turned to Troy.

"Sleep," he said.

Troy didn't go down.

Edward darted forward while Troy continued lifting

a gleam of silver flashing under the moonlight. A crucifix.

Unfortunately, Edward was faster than Troy.

Time throttled back to its regular pace and, before Kim knew it, her coworker was slumped on the ground and Edward was holding up two earplugs like trophies.

"Hats off to this," the rogue said.

He opened his mouth to say something else, but instead, cocked his head, as if hearing something.

Stephen?

Oh, God, she sensed him. Somewhere, he was somewhere near.

Before she could get too giddy, Edward motioned toward her.

"Sleep."

The world closed into pinpoints, disappearing on the gasp of her heart as she thought *Stephen* for the last time.

Her body waved while ecstasy took her under into the thick, fluid blackness of limbo.

PRIDE, Stephen had thought over and over again as he used his senses to search for the old gas station and the rogue. *I have too much pride. I should have unburdened myself before leaving her. Better yet, I should have…*

Done what? Allowed Kimberly to come along?

Inconceivable. So why did he regret not doing it?

When he arrived at the station, then found it empty, he cursed himself, knowing only then exactly what was happening.

He had been duped.

In a panic, he zipped back to League headquarters, hoping his suspicions were wrong.

But then he caught her scent in the desert behind the house, just as if she were a part of him, and his gut fisted. He sighted a man's form standing near a cluster of prone humans.

Yet Kimberly's body was all that registered in Stephen's mind before it went red and garbled.

Without another thought, he tensed, shooting toward the scene, never heeding what might happen to himself.

Even as he zoomed downward, his heightened vision fixed on the rogue as the other vampire kneeled over Kimberly and poised his hand over her chest.

Bloody... This rogue wasn't intending to bite her this time. He was going to tear her heart out.

Stephen wouldn't be able to heal that sort of damage.

Burning to a halt in midair, Stephen hovered, attempting to keep himself together, though he was on the cusp of imploding. "Stand away from her."

His voice came out as a dangerous growl.

The rogue raised his head, revealing his face.

Stephen jerked, as if gutted. Such a familiar face, such a dear missed brother.

"Edward," he said.

The other vampire tried to smile at Stephen, as if to conjure old times and grand days. Edward Marburn—literally, a bastard, born to a duke and left to fend for himself with a sick mother; a good friend who always watched Stephen's back, whether during a road robbery or a more subtle con job; a comrade missing in action just before the start of the Second World War.

Like their other close vampire brother, Roger, Edward had undergone a crisis of conscience when Stephen turned bitter after Cassandra had torn the figurative heart from him. He had began to study world religion and philosophy, undergoing a severe case of self-loathing even worse than Stephen's. However, unlike his brothers, Edward had come to actively despise Fegan for turning him into a vampire, so he had broken from the gang's clutches under Fegan's threat of decapitation if he ever encountered the gang again.

Seeing Edward using Kimberly, *his* Kimberly, as a shield for the second night in a row, Stephen's flesh twisted. His fangs speared from his gums. His face reshaped into what he knew to be a monstrosity.

He became the horror he detested—a form he couldn't deny in his rage.

"If you harm her," Stephen snarled, "I'll tear you limb from limb."

"That's some welcome." Edward had been teased for his pretty face often enough, and he had used his male-steeped beauty to great advantage many a time. But now he was hideous, perverse in his fall from grace. "I'd wished for a friendlier hello, Stephen."

"You didn't encourage it."

All he could see was Kimberly, her red hair spread over the ground, her eyes closed in peaceful repose, her chest just under Edward's clawed hand.

Then her neck…her lovely, vulnerable neck.

The saliva went hot in Stephen's mouth, even as he denied how she lured him.

Edward caught on to his brother's struggles. "She really is enough to melt a heart like yours, isn't she?"

An injured gasp sounded from the right, and Stephen saw Kimberly's friend, Darlene, shooting Edward a betrayed glare from her waiting spot near a hill. The other vampire ignored her, instead concentrating on the still-hovering Stephen.

Yet Edward's words were ringing through air that was too thick, too hard to breathe. *To melt a heart like yours.*

But Stephen had no heart, no emotion.

No. *No.*

The protestations held no conviction because Stephen knew he could not deny his affection for Kimberly any longer. He had never wanted a human more, never wanted the agony of needing her like he did at this moment.

Edward clearly recognized this, and he repositioned himself above Kimberly for an attack. She was his leverage once again. He must have captivated her and the others just after Stephen had left in such greedy haste to find the rogue.

He guessed Darlene had much to do with luring Kimberly out here, as well.

"What do you want of me, Edward?" Stephen asked, his voice slashing through his throat.

"There we go." The rogue—his old friend, for mercy's sake—didn't move from his vicious pose. Yet his voice held no rancor, only something like exhaustion. "All I want is for you to hear me out, Stephen. Please, brother. *Please.*"

His words were so soaked in desperation that Stephen found himself listening. How could he not with Edward? He had always been a thoughtful man, and that was why it had been so terrible to see his descent into hatred, then his shameful exodus.

"Why?" Stephen asked. "Why have you been draining these women? Why Darlene? Why—" his blood began boiling as he drank in the sight of Kimberly "—this?"

Edward paused, as if to measure how close Stephen was to attacking. But he must have realized his old friend would do nothing to endanger Kimberly, so he relaxed, though he didn't cease from threatening her.

The resulting snap of relief wasn't enough to set Stephen at peace because this wasn't even close to over.

Kimberly, he kept thinking, *I won't allow you to suffer in any way. I will do anything, anything at all.*

His heart pumped dread through him, and the sensation was fresh and raw. He felt alive, certainly—every inch, every cell. But, this time, it was a terrible thing.

Edward spoke again. "Since leaving the gang, I've spent years despising this curse of mine. Of *ours.*"

The reminder made Stephen sink closer to the ground, but he remained perched on air, alert.

"I've thought long and hard about what should be done," Edward continued. "About what's just and right."

"Just and right? Fegan never taught us any of that."

"I know." Edward's eyes gleamed with malice. "Funny how humans believe monsters in fairy tales are figments of the imagination. If only they knew our master walked among them, they would never sleep at night."

It sounded as if Edward had decided Fegan was the sole source of their misery. Perhaps it was even true.

Yet Stephen had always known he could leave the gang at any time, just as Edward had. However, love him or not, Fegan was their father—part of the family Stephen had always told himself he needed.

Edward laid his fingers on Kimberly's chest, and Stephen bristled.

"What are you trying to tell me, Edward?" he spat, too helpless, too attached, too beaten by emotion to know how to handle this mess besides proceeding warily. "What does all this have to do with those women you attacked?"

The rogue's eyes went sorrowful. "I've tried to find Fegan. I've looked high and low, but he is a master—a master of hiding, of shielding. All of you are."

"That is how we never got caught. Not for any of our crimes."

"But we should have. We should have gotten caught and punished, Stephen."

The remorse he had begun to feel of late was apparent in Edward's eyes. In spite of himself, Stephen empathized fully.

"Brother," the nobleman said softly, "I don't want to hurt her."

He motioned to Kimberly.

Edward was begging, but it was not enough to put Stephen off his guard.

"Then, all you have to do is leave her to me, Edward. I'll listen, if you only let her go."

"If you vow to give me Fegan, she is yours."

The blasphemous request shook Stephen enough to make him drop to the ground, where he landed with a stumble.

Edward tilted his head. "I want to be free, to be human again. To start over. That's all I've wanted for years now. Haven't you thought about it, too, Stephen? Haven't you ever recalled what it was like to feel the sun and to be so happy in its warmth that you didn't know if you could stand it? And our crimes… I'm not talking about the petty things we did in our mortal days, but what we committed under Fegan's instruction. The murders, the feedings, how many lives we must have ruined. I want to redeem myself by doing the only task that can possibly make up for them—ridding this world of Fegan's stench."

Stephen's head was swirling. Kimberly had taught him just how destructive his bite could be to a human. He had sinned beyond redemption—or so he had believed, because he didn't know any way to seek a new beginning. But Edward was talking of the profane, the unthinkable, as a way to cleanse themselves.

"You wish to kill your own creator so you might become human again?" Stephen asked on a warped whisper.

Edward nodded, eyes going back to that piercing gleam, like a knife hidden just under a black cape. "It's the only way."

"Killing a master and having that result in his children becoming human is merely a myth."

"No." The rogue emphatically shook his head. "I've seen it come true during my travels, with other vampire families. It's the only way I know of to become mortal again, to start a new life and leave the sins in the past."

In his anguish, Edward had tightened his fingers on Kimberly's tank top. Stephen's gut lurched, and he growled in warning.

Apologetically, the other vampire loosened his hold, yet still remained in attack position.

Stephen tried to recover from the very thought of patricide; it was disdainful yet horrifyingly righteous, now that Edward was speaking of it. In the back of his mind, he had pictured bringing Fegan to justice many a time, especially while the creator reveled in his tales of unneeded bloodletting. Stephen and his brothers had, indeed, been rascals themselves, but they had stopped kilometers short of Fegan's own isolated activities, hence forcing their father to sate his more unsavory appetites on his own.

It made no sense to stop murder with another murder.

Still, at the same time, he had wondered when and how Fegan would ever get his comeuppance.

Now, as Edward brought his idea of justice to light, Stephen listened, compelled yet torn.

"Until now," the rogue said, "I've been unsuccessful in isolating Fegan's exact whereabouts. I tracked him to Las Vegas only a month ago, but there are so many hiding places here. The civilized vampire areas are confused by the presence of other creatures, and I attempted to sort them all out. But there was never a Fegan, never a sign of our gang that I could hold on to. And other creatures wouldn't talk about him to strangers—that's because they knew what would happen if they did. Fegan wields a reputation for destruction. No matter where he goes, he's in charge, even from the ether where he's cowering."

Stephen fixed his gaze on Kimberly, the one reason he was not rotting apart, piece by piece, right now. How could he get Edward away from this woman he had come to treasure in such a short time?

His determination to do anything to get her back reasserted itself. He wanted to see her brilliant eyes flashing with such life, to feel her against him conjuring the heat he couldn't seem to sustain within himself. He wanted to feel the emotions only she brought out in him; *she* could take him away from all this ugliness. Only Kimberly.

He tried his best not to allow Edward to see just how much of Stephen he was holding captive.

"Therefore," Stephen said evenly, not betraying his true crumbling state, "you began draining victims in order to gain Fegan's attention? And I can only surmise that you've charmed Darlene into your services, as well."

Edward glanced at the woman staring at him from the

hill. "Yes, pity, that. When I heard around town that you were in with this Van Helsing League, which was easily found on the Internet, I did my research. I read that my darling Darlene would be patrolling Mystique, looking for me. Poor naif. When the drainings weren't working as quickly as I would've liked, I tried to arrange our first private meeting through her, you know, by setting her up at the construction site where she would most likely lure you. Yet you brought *this* hunter with you, this redhead."

"Kimberly," Stephen said, her name catching in his throat.

Edward scanned his leverage, then sighed. "I didn't drain Darlene, only used her to perform such tasks as planting tonight's e-mail, knowing your Kimberly would pass the information on to you and we would all meet again under circumstances more beneficial to my cause."

Stephen quelled his rising anger, mainly culled from the tender way Edward was looking at Kimberly—as if he envied Stephen the emotion he had invested in her.

"And all the other women?" Stephen asked, his voice stabbing.

"The others." Edward reluctantly glanced away from Kimberly. "I knew drainings would interest every local vampire; it would strike fear into every local master. If Fegan didn't come out to play himself—which was likely for a coward—he would send one of his most trusted in his place so that I could be brought to court before His Honor and tried accordingly. I hoped the enforcer would be you or Roger."

"And you believed we would hear you out and perhaps even come to your side."

"Yes." Edward's smile shook with the effort. "Because I know you, Stephen. You and Roger—maybe even Henry and Rupert—hate what you are as much as I do, and you despise

Fegan for it, whether you admit it or not. No one, not even a vampire, can remain loyal to a thing like Fegan forever."

Something caught Stephen's attention—a flicker near Kimberly's hand. It was one of her fingers twitching.

Pure joy threaded through him, twining all his loose feelings until he was held together in gathered strength. In hope.

But there was something still weighing on him.

Edward wished to kill Fegan and become human—consequently turning every one of Fegan's children human, as well.

Yet Kimberly craved the *vampire* in Stephen. Not the man.

If Stephen chose to go along with Edward in this plan to redeem all of them—a plan that ripped Stephen in two—he would be like any other man to Kimberly, no longer a vampire.

No longer enough to enthrall her.

Losing her mattered—mattered too much for him to withstand. Losing her meant a return to true darkness.

Stephen sought to distract Edward from his awakening victim. "Why didn't you merely send word to the community that you wished an audience with Fegan? He might have called off his death vow against you and entertained your presence until you could attempt an attack on him. He might have considered that amusing."

"Oh, Stephen, it wasn't just about finding him." Edward sighed. "It was about punishing him for the cruelty he's enjoyed. He's never learned what's right, and he'll always be there, on the dark side of every tragedy, to laugh and continue on to the next one. Has he felt any impotence during my attacks? Has he squirmed even the slightest bit?"

Stephen's silence said everything.

"Then, I've done half my job, already," Edward concluded.

"And while you've been carrying out your vendetta, you've harmed more victims in the process." Stephen's throat had almost closed around the words.

He had to do something, anything to get Kimberly away from Edward. Last time had just been a warning bite. This time, if Edward felt that Stephen had turned against him…

Even in the flash it would take for Stephen to get to Kimberly's side, Edward would have the speed to carry out a fatal strike.

At the mere thought, Stephen died a little inside.

"I'll let her go if you vow to give me Fegan," Edward repeated.

Stephen jerked, as if yanked in Fegan's compelling direction out of habit and bent loyalty, even as he clung to Kimberly. "How can you ask such a thing?"

"Please, Stephen. This is only a means to an end. Please don't make me hurt her."

But Stephen knew that his ex-gang member would do it. Blood was part of their existence, and spilling one more drop to balance the scales of justice would not matter to Edward at this point.

"Please," his old friend whispered.

Stephen closed his gaze. But when the image of Kimberly refused to fade from his mind's eye, he knew that there was no decision to make at all. Even if she awoke to find him mortal and unappealing, Stephen knew how this had to end.

Even if it meant losing her—losing the ability to feel reborn.

He tried not to think about how she might actually move on to the next vampire for its bite. She thrived on the sexual power, and he understood an addiction more than anyone.

But he would not be able to provide for her anymore.

To erase the devastation, Stephen attempted to think of what good being human again would do. He could redeem himself. He would not live on and on with the knowledge that Kimberly had turned him away just as Cassandra had; he would only have to endure the pain for years instead of centuries.

Edward clearly didn't appreciate the process of Stephen breaking down, bone by bone. He reared back a hand, intent on digging it into Kimberly—

"No!" Stephen yelled.

Edward pulled back, a sublime expression of relief on his face.

Horror at the thought of Kimberly's death pushed the exact location of the canyon hideout out of Stephen's lungs. And while he revealed every detail of Fegan's whereabouts, all the resentment he held for his master surfaced, as if it could take the place of the hope draining from his body. Every repressed memory impaled him, spilling guilt into the emptiness losing Kimberly had already left.

He recalled tales of what Fegan had done—gutting a tavern maid back in York so he could bury himself in her blood; torturing a young boy in Florence just to laugh at his screams…

Yes, this was the right choice, though Stephen would gain—and lose—everything after Kimberly realized what had happened.

After receiving what he wanted, Edward bowed to Stephen, then stood, backing away from Kimberly. Tears glinted on his face like glass wishes falling to be broken.

Stephen darted to her, holding her, so many unnameable emotions swarming inside him that he felt *too* much. As a result, he pressed her hard against him, and she gasped.

Last moments, he thought. *This woman is going to stop wanting me as soon as Edward—*

"Awaken," the other vampire said to each sleeper, then split the night air in flight.

Darlene ran from the small hill to cry out at Edward's departure. Then she sank to the ground, weeping, no doubt knowing she had only been used.

Kimberly was trying to choke out words.

"Shh," Stephen said, brushing the hair back from her forehead, prizing these final moments if Edward should be successful in his quest. "Just rest, my love. Just let me hold you."

His blood raced at the terrible thought of freedom, at the cost of it. After he turned, she would see him as any other man who had disappointed her. He would no longer be the dazzling creature who could woo with escapism and a false sense of joy.

"I heard—" she licked her lips, her eyes dark with fear "—I heard everything. What did you do, Stephen?"

His eyes filled with liquid heat. "Kimberly, he would have killed you, and I couldn't bear it."

"Your family—" she gathered strength, fire "—your *existence.*"

His vampire. She was already mourning its passing.

"Stephen…" A tear slid out of her eye.

Clearly, she had found a real-life fantasy—one that had

brought her so much ecstasy—and it was going to be destroyed before her very eyes.

And *his* eyes.

The realization ripped at him, but as that rip turned into a full-blown tear, as if he were physically being rent in two, Stephen reared back his head and yelled at the agony of Edward having already succeeded in his quest.

14

EDWARD HAD NEVER flown faster, and as he followed Stephen's detailed directions, his vampiric speed and finesse led him straight to the canyon, through its trenches and tunnels, then to Fegan.

The other members of the gang hadn't even the time to gasp as Edward zipped straight for their creator and materialized before the old vampire, who was sitting on a velvet throne.

A long second passed as Edward stood there, panting, waiting for Fegan to recognize him. Finally, even before the other creature's sight focused, Edward's masked scent flared Fegan's nostrils.

Edward smiled.

"*Damn* you," Edward said, just before pulling a short sword out of the scabbard hidden by his coat. He struck without another thought.

The creator's mouth opened in surprise, but Edward's aim had been true to Fegan's neck. The blow turned the glutton completely to a dust that showered like dirty rain over the velvet.

It was that easy.

Edward only had time enough to hear the shouts of the gang and to feel as if he had removed a cancer from the center of him before he convulsed, falling before the empty throne in a mockery of respect for Fegan.

Yet, before everything scrambled inside his brain, before his vision rolled and his body screeched apart, Edward thought of how Stephen's human woman had looked upon him just after awakening, and how Stephen had looked upon her while believing she was going to die.

The power of their connection rocked Edward into a place where the pain existed outside, not inside. Instead, he felt suspended, floating as his body had been reborn to what it once was.

He found his humanity in a way Stephen had obviously not required, and he groaned at the necessity of it.

At the glorious coming of it.

Eventually, in what seemed like a break in time, everything coalesced, and Edward opened his eyes. Emotion—such true clarity that he could not recognize what he was feeling—rushed upon him. Choking up, he rose to a seated position, taking in the cavern and all its spoils—the excessive chandelier, the rich velvet curtains and portraits. The colors were faded to an eye that was used to vibrancy, but for Edward, the muted hues were heartbreakingly beautiful.

And his hearing…his ears were no longer pierced with the excruciating overkill of everyday sounds. No, there was only drawn-out moaning as the rest of his brothers arose from their lounging areas around the cave. Roger and Henry both inspected their hands in wonder. Rupert touched his chest and let out a belly laugh. Had Edward actually done right by them in terminating their creator?

Only Little Sam wore a crushed scowl as he wobbled to a stand and fell back to his hands and knees. He began to sob.

Human. They were all wonderfully human.

On a broken cry, Edward weakly got to his knees, reaching out to touch Fegan's deserted throne. He wished to feel the velvet against his skin, to feel the change in everything around him. To feel—*feel!* It was all so new, so breathtaking.

But, without warning, a scream crushed the serenity, and something flew at him from across the cavern.

Before Edward's perception settled, he found a black-haired female hunched over him, hellfire in her light brown eyes and fangs gleaming as she hissed.

Who was she? A new member initiated after Edward had left the gang? So why hadn't she changed, too?

"Murderer," she said in a garbled tone. *"Murderer!"*

"It is a reckoning." Edward's pulse thudded. Now that he was mortal, he had no defenses, no powers.

"It is an assassination."

Through her anger, he could see great sadness, as if she genuinely mourned that bastard Fegan.

Edward wished he had the strength to convey what would happen to her after she had lived long enough like this. One night, she would realize the truth about her family—their dysfunction born of an evil patriarch. Like him, she would start to take her victims' blood peacefully out of pure guilt until more dire actions were required to seek justice. Or she might study the philosophies of diverse cultures while attempting to find truth—any truth—in how she was made to exist in this way.

But right now, in her grief, this angry vampire was threatening to destroy what he had worked so hard to bring about. She had a killing despair in her gaze, and he needed to persuade her that he'd improved her existence, not made it worse.

Yet, before he could begin, she cocked her head.

"I think you are one of them," she said, her speech slightly accented with a French poison. "You are a deserter."

"I'm *Edward.*" A man. A human, for God's sake. Finally human!

As she arched above him, her eyes taking on even more rage, he could hear the rest of the gang hanging back. There was even a steel rattle, as if perhaps one or more of them were gathering weapons. They would need those to take the place of their preternatural powers if they wished to face this wounded female.

At least, Edward chose to believe they were going to use them on this vampire rather than on him.

The female's lips twitched. "You never appreciated what Fegan gave you. He gave the same to me, even though he did not bear me."

No… Oh, no… She hadn't become mortal because killing Fegan had no effect on a vampire who wasn't his child.

"You are an ingrate." Her voice shook. "And you took my savior. You took what he gave so freely."

The rest of her sentence was implicit: *You deserve to be punished for my loss.*

Just as he'd sought to punish Fegan for his own.

As he saw the tragic irony, she lashed out in her own act of vengeance, sinking her teeth into his neck. Then she drew her own blood with a slash of a nail to her chest so quickly that he didn't even have time to resist her in this new human state, to push back before she forced his mouth to her wound.

The blood entered his system like a virus, spreading, altering, bringing back the painful colors and sounds.

With just one bite, everything around him became a scream that shattered every last one of his dreams.

WHILE STEPHEN WRITHED on the desert ground and clutched in agony, Kim reached for him, not knowing what to do to make it stop. She would do *anything* to make it stop.

"Stephen," she said, panicking. "Oh, my God…"

The other awakened members of the League had gathered around, too. Powder was holding a cognizant Darlene back as if she might cause more trouble.

But then, as fast as it'd started, it was over. Just like that—a tornado that had spent itself and died.

A whipped Stephen lay on the sand, arms and legs spread, his long hair covering most of his face. It was then, in the aftermath, that Kim realized Edward had made good on his ambitions and killed their creator.

Her blood chilled.

Stephen was…

No. He couldn't be. Even in her Edward-controlled "sleep" she'd heard everything, as if in a fever dream. Still, she couldn't grasp the meaning of what she was seeing.

"He's gone human," Troy whispered from behind her.

Shocked by the sound of a voice entering her confusion, Kim's glance sought her cohunter, who'd clearly heard everything, too.

He seemed so sympathetic. "I suspected all along. But it was obvious Stephen wasn't out to do damage. He would've shut all of us up properly, right away, if he wanted to."

One thing went unsaid by Troy: *But I watched. I waited. Just in case.*

Kim turned back to Stephen. The moonlight washed

over him, and she touched him tentatively, brushing the hair from his face. She sucked in a breath.

He had lost his… She guessed it could be called *sheen*. No more preternatural gloss, just a broken and bruised man.

No one said a word. Not until Troy backed away, then halted, waiting for the rest of his group.

"Let's leave them alone, guys," he said.

One by one, they did, though Powder was holding a contrite Darlene as she began to sob. Troy was the last to go, laying a sorry glance on Kim before he turned and followed his League members.

That left her with the empty sounds of the night desert, the hush of air going still.

When she looked back at Stephen, he had opened his eyes and was watching her.

Neither of them said anything.

How could she? It was enough to absorb how his gaze was less of a blazing green and now…softer. Where the color had been a heated cool, now it was tinted with trepidation. His stark emotion drew her in a way it hadn't before, yet it also scared her to death.

God. She was afraid of him now, so much more afraid than when he'd been a so-called monster.

As if they were living a bad morning after, Stephen turned his back on her and rose to a sitting position. He hunched, defensive, beaten.

"So Edward did it," Kim said.

Stephen's voice was ragged. "Yes. I seem to have become…" He laughed, but it was a sound of pain.

This had to be a shock for him, even though she suspected that he'd contained more humanity than he'd realized, all along.

"You're a man," she said, "an actual man now."

"A man," he repeated, but with more venom than she'd ever heard in her life.

She'd always sensed that a part of him hated what he'd become. So wasn't this an opportunity for him to right all the wrongs he seemed so sorry for? Wasn't this good?

She could only sit there. When he chanced a glance back at her, something seemed to crack in him. He assumed the fury of a man who didn't care what he said anymore. A man who'd lost everything even though he'd gained so much.

"I'm now what you rejected in every other male you've been with since that first bite, Kimberly. I'm what you have been running from. So how do I look to you—like another fantasy come true?"

As she fumbled for something to say, he clearly took her silence for something else. He got to his feet, although, it was without his usual self-confidence.

That lack of arrogance seemed to squeeze every last drop of blood out of her heart. He was accessible now, the representation of everything that was fleeting about life, everything that could be snatched away in one traumatic moment.

Still, as he took a step away, she grabbed at his long coat. "Where do you think you're going?"

"Away. Anywhere. I don't wish to prolong this."

"Prolong what?" She shook her head, angry at herself for continuing to play this game when she should be laying everything out right now. Isn't that what she'd wanted to do back when Edward had been threatening her?

Standing, she held fast to his coat, but he moved away from her, nonetheless, heading in the direction of the old shed. The canvas at the structure's side beat fruitlessly against the broken frame.

"Stephen!"

He halted, as if commanded. My God, there wasn't anything vampiric left, yet she still had some kind of power over him.

Why?

"I don't want you to go," she whispered.

His chest was rising and falling with the force of his breathing. "But I *have* gone, Kimberly. The vampire is dead, and there are no more bites in your future. Not with me."

"Is that what you think?" She laughed, but without mirth. "And here I thought I wasn't the only one who wanted—" a bolt of fear cut her off, but she was sick of holding back "—who wanted more. Hell, I thought there *was* more to us."

"I'm not what you want anymore. I can't give you what you crave from me."

The night shifted around them; the moon hid behind a bank of clouds.

Stephen continued, "I gave Edward what he needed because he had you at his mercy. Having to see your life ended…it was not an option. It would have killed me as surely as any weapon."

Wait. She couldn't get this through her head. "You did this for me? Not because you wanted to be human again? It was for *me?*"

"You seem to be the reason for everything, Kimberly. At least, you were."

She *was.* What did he think—that she was going to drop him because he couldn't bite her anymore?

Then again, why shouldn't he think that, with the way she'd been pursuing bites like a girl in demented heat?

Once more, a zap of fear adrenalized her. Ridiculous. Stephen had made an impossible decision that told her everything about what he felt for her, yet she was still afraid.

Why? Because now, in human form, he was everything she'd turned her back on when he'd bitten her that first time. He symbolized commitment and handing your heart over to another person's care. He could give her what Lori had taken away—the trust you put in another person when you loved them.

But, as he'd once pointed out, this was a different kind of love, one she'd never allowed herself to indulge in before. It was far more vital, alive in its potential for anguish, passionate to the point of losing your soul.

What would happen if she gave in to it? Just look at the tailspin she'd gone into after Lori's death. What would it do to her to lose a mate who had shown her a new world, one that didn't necessarily have anything to do with the preternatural?

She didn't know what to do; but then again, she really did. She needed to stop him from leaving, from taking the simple yet all-important happiness she'd found with him.

"Even though you don't have those great powers, anymore," she said, "you can probably see it in my eyes. I'm terrified, Stephen."

He looked confused at the irony—she hadn't run away from his monster, but now that he was a man, she was ready to turn tail and dash.

"This is all new for me, too." He reached up, hesitated, then indicated her sand-scrubbed arm. "I don't even have healing powers."

She swallowed at the sadness in his eyes. Then, as if encouraged by that, he stroked his knuckles over her chest, where her shirt revealed flesh and her heart thumped.

"But this…" he said. "Your skin. It's just as soft as it was before. That hasn't changed. Neither has what's beneath your skin, I hope. But again—" he dragged his fingers to her throat, over her jugular "—I don't know how to handle my hunger for you now."

She wasn't sure how to handle him, either. Fantasies were so easy, because you could just tuck them away when they were over. But this…*this?*

Her heart tapped against her chest, a message from a more rational part of her that wasn't absolutely in control yet. "I guess we could try to find out how to deal with what's happened to us together. We made a good team before, right?"

At his disappointed reaction to her light comment, he turned away, entering the shack's entrance and pushing back the canvas as a final, symbolic closure.

But she surged forward, into the shack, clinging to him.

She wasn't letting him go. Couldn't. Wouldn't.

With a groan, he cradled her, and they dropped to their knees, then looked down at her, the first spark of hope lighting his eyes as the moon uncovered itself again. It seeped through the slats of the canvas just enough to provide illumination.

"I was missing something with every bite," she said, starting to shake in earnest. "*You.* The real Stephen. I kept seeing flashes of that inside of you, but I didn't realize…"

He merely skimmed her hair back from her face, as if drinking her in.

"Your bite made me feel like I was your everything," she added, "and I always wanted that, no matter how scared I was. To be *someone*'s everything."

"Funny." Stephen laid his fingers over her lips, his touch seeming to scorch her. "I didn't have to bite you to feel that way. You got into my blood without my having to taste it. You took me over."

She finally allowed herself to believe it—to believe in *him*. His words were like a cloak wrapped around her, one of those magic ones that kids pretend to use for invisibility or safety. But hers was woven from his sincerity. She'd been in his head and knew him as completely as she could ever want—as completely as a cloak would cover her from now on.

She leaned forward, resting her mouth against his. There was no hint of fangs this time as they breathed against each other, warm, moist tingles of promise.

"You're so real," she said against his lips, running a hand down his chest.

His body wasn't as hard, yet it wasn't soft, either. Stephen was fit and lithe, an animal made for activity. She stripped off his coat so she could explore more.

After all this, she didn't need to prove anything to herself, didn't need a bite for diversion or even reassurance.

Her pulse picked up speed, tapping, tapping. But now she understood what her body was trying to say—she'd hunted for a vampire, but found herself, instead, in the man he had become.

Once she got his coat off, she went to work on his shirt, tearing at it, tossing it away in anticipation of testing his skin with her palms.

"You're rougher to the touch," she said, skimming over his bare chest, its firmness and contours. "I like that. I like it a lot."

He'd been waiting patiently, but it was only when she caught his heated gaze that she realized he'd been watching her the whole time. For a second, she saw a wild craving there, reminding her of what he used to be.

Of how much she still mattered to him.

He hadn't lost what had attracted her in the first place. That drove her on, and she attacked the top button of his pants. Everything about him was fueling her—the musky smell just beginning to emanate from him, the more primal feel of his skin.

"Do you remember what it was like to make love as a human?" she asked.

He grabbed her wrists just as she parted his fly and exposed his shaft. It was veined and engorged.

"You're the only woman I can think about now."

With that, he raised her hands above her head, then slowly peeled her tank top up and off.

Stephen reached behind her to unhook her lacy bra. When her breasts tumbled free, he couldn't stop lavishing them with his gaze, even as he dropped the material and pressed her hands behind her back.

His body had far less control now, and it pounded with the blood coursing through every inch of him. Most of it gushed to his cock, which had pushed its way out of his trousers and was bobbing in stimulation.

Reverently, he placed his palms over her belly, enjoying the sensation of his rougher hands over her smooth skin. He slid upward, over her belly ring, over the curve of her waist, her ribs, all in lingering madness.

When he got to her breasts, full and ripe, he held their weight, painting her nipples by circling his thumbs there.

Kimberly leaned back her head, exposing her neck. But

there was no blood hunger at the sight; no, he wanted the *more* they had been talking of. Wanted something he had never devoured before because it hadn't fully emerged yet.

"Maybe the colors around you are not as impressive as they were earlier," he whispered in her ear, "but you have not changed in my eyes, Kimberly. You're just as enchanting."

He moved to kiss her, to sip and to taste. Slipping his hands to the small of her back, he pressed her against him. Her bare breasts smashed against his chest, her nipples beaded and slick against a sheen of perspiration that had begun to coat him.

These new, less refined, but just as potent sensations sent a blast of heat all over him, and his cock nudged her belly. As they sucked at each other's lips, drawing out the kiss in long, sensual strokes, he used one hand to work at her fly. When he had it undone, he eased his fingers inside her underwear, parting her legs, then her curls to get at the humid folds of her.

Slow, thorough. He took his time, listening to her wince against his mouth, feeling her hips shift with his every motion. She pushed down her jeans, giving him more access, allowing him to work her clitoris, then coax his fingers up into her.

She lightly bit his bottom lip, then as she sucked it, tightened her muscles around his fingers in playful insinuation.

Clenching, loosening. Each time she relaxed, he thrust harder. Soon, his fingers were sopping, busy with bringing her to moaning weakness.

"There could be a bigger part of you inside," she said with effort, reaching down to grasp his penis.

It throbbed, and a tiny spurt wet his tip. He knew that, now, everything was different. He was alive—every part of him.

Everything.

They stripped, and he hauled her against him, mindful of the concrete floor and her comfort. While he took his position on the ground, reveling in the burn scratching at his legs and ass, she climbed on his lap, wrapping her legs around him.

She teased him more, skimming her sex over his cock, drenching his head with her juices. His sensitive tip slicked through her folds, pressing against the bud until she groaned.

Then, as if executing her own revenge, she drew back and impaled herself on his thudding erection.

She gave a thrilled cry and rolled her hips, enclosing him in silken wetness, in a tunnel with a pinpoint of light beckoning at the end.

"My Stephen," she said, churning as he held her hips.

He worked her around and around while his vision collapsed before him.

He was speeding through that tunnel, the light becoming nearer, brighter, as the walls sucked in on him. His skin felt pressurized, and he buried his face in her neck, her hair fragrant, her skin earthy with sex and sweat.

Pounding, pounding—he beat toward the tunnel's end, the light burning, heating, flaring until he couldn't look at it anymore.

She stiffened, crying out, but he kept going, losing himself against her, in her.

A fleeting eternity whirled by, and his body convulsed, then seemed to explode. The light consumed him, throwing him backward, forward, everywhere.

Gasping, he tasted her skin as he came to, his mouth on her neck as he heaved in oxygen, which seemed to have been depleted from the atmosphere only moments earlier.

As they held each other, the sky paled, introducing sunlight on its rise as it peeked through the shack's canvas.

It warmed all the years he would have with the woman who whispered "My Stephen" in his ear before she buried her face in his neck and bit it lightly.

Epilogue

A YEAR HAD PASSED with astounding speed, but only because happiness had a tendency to fly faster than days full of fear.

It was nighttime, and Kim rested on the porch of the cabin she and Stephen had bought in Big Bear, near Los Angeles. It was cozy and isolated. Nestled amongst the late-summer trees, they didn't have much cause to realize that civilization was just a short drive away.

No, here every turning leaf told its own story, every flash off the lake's water hinted at the gorgeous details that life had to offer every single day.

She heard the sound of tires crunching on gravel, and lazily turned her head toward their expected visitor as garage lights flooded the drive.

Edward. He had contacted Stephen earlier this week and would be staying in their guestroom downstairs. What he didn't know was that Stephen had invited Edward over to seriously talk. In his continued quest to find humanity, Edward risked falling into deeper hatred.

In a spirit of rebirth, both she and Stephen were working on forgiving the ex-gang member for threatening Kim, which wasn't easy. Still, they both thought forgiveness was essential to starting over with a clean slate, so here

Edward was, the vampire seeking absolution who constantly phoned their home to apologize for what he'd done.

As Kim watched her husband and Edward greet each other and then head for the porch, she sighed. Stephen was just as hot as he had been as a vamp. Sure, he didn't move as gracefully, but he still glided like a sleek animal. And he didn't have that "sheen," but he was even more masculine without it. Truthfully, he hadn't changed all that much except for the obvious happiness that outlined his body like an aura only she could see.

Physically, she had changed, too, though her added weight gain was a few pounds for the way, way better. She'd realized that the confidence she'd gained from his bites was permanent, but that was only because he loved her and she loved him, so carrying herself with ease wasn't a challenge.

She got to her feet, her rocker moaning against the floorboards, and set aside the postcard she'd gotten from Powder and Darlene while they traveled the Swiss Alps. After Darlene had gotten over Edward's treatment of her— something made possible when he'd apologized to her, as well, earlier this year—she'd taken up with Powder. Of course, Edward's spell had dissipated when he'd gone human for a short time, so Darlene was free of him, just as vampires at large were free of the Van Helsing League.

The group had broken apart after the near tragic confrontation. Troy had said that Stephen made him realize something—that exposing the breed meant hurting the decent vamps who were genuinely trying to police themselves, ones such as Stephen.

"Hey, Edward," she said, embracing him.

He was just as wiry as usual, and that translated into a

lethal agility he needed to hunt down the vampire, Gisele, who had ruined his dreams of mortality. In spite of his efforts to make everything up to those he'd hurt during his search for Fegan, Edward was smack in the middle of a second vendetta. The rest of the ex-gang—Roger, Henry and Rupert—were living well and prospering, and they'd all met with Edward one time or another in an effort to see if there was another solution to finding happiness for their old comrade.

But there wasn't. Edward still had his mission, no matter how bitter it was. He was intent on catching his new creator, Gisele, plus Little Sam, who'd convinced her to return him to a vampiric state, too. Making her pay with death was the only way Edward could become human again, though he seemed to be missing the bigger picture. He could *act* human, even if he was a vampire.

Stephen had known this, yet even he admitted that being mortal and loving Kim on more normal terms was a great gift.

"Good to see you, Kimberly," Edward said, backing away from her and stuffing his hands in his trouser pockets.

And then he smiled—a bright, sweet, sad smile—and she knew he saw the piece of furniture behind her.

As he went over to the cradle, Stephen's gaze caught Kim's. It was as if the floor moved under her feet, shifting until her body felt dismantled from the force.

"I love you," her husband mouthed.

Then everything pieced itself back together within her, a beautiful stained-glass window that glowed.

"I love you, too," she whispered right back.

Edward was shaking his head as he looked at Stephen and Kim's child swathed in his cradle. "He's beautiful."

"Sorry Nate's sleeping right now," she said. "But he'll

be up and about pretty early, probably just before you settle into some slumber, yourself."

Edward reached out, then pulled his hand back, as if afraid to touch the infant at all. Kim had known that feeling—a lost sense of fear that could freeze you into the wrong life.

But Stephen had shown her how to embrace what she wanted, even while knowing that it all could disappear at any time. The key was in appreciating it while you could. There wasn't any more she could do than that, so every second was precious.

She went to her husband and latched on to him. He held just as tightly to her as they watched Edward inspect Nate. Stephen didn't need to be a vampire to glow, because he was doing a good job of it now—their son was the ultimate proof of life as he'd longed for it.

At that moment, Nate woke up and shined a smile at Edward, who looked stunned to be so affected by a little baby.

Pressing her face into Stephen's chest and feeling his arms around her, Kim saw forever in her son, in those trees surrounding them, in the moon-glittered lake.

In the embrace of her husband.

And maybe, someday, they could help Edward find the rest of forever, too.

* * * * *

Every Life Has More
Than One Chapter

Award-winning author Stevi Mittman delivers
another hysterical mystery, featuring Teddi Bayer, an
irrepressible heroine, and her to-die-for hero, Detective Drew Scoones. After all, life on Long Island can
be murder!

*Turn the page for a sneak peek at the
warm and funny fourth book,
WHOSE NUMBER IS UP, ANYWAY?,
in the Teddi Bayer series,
by STEVI MITTMAN.
On sale August 7*

CHAPTER 1

"Before redecorating a room, I always advise my clients to empty it of everything but one chair. Then I suggest they move that chair from place to place, sitting in it, until the placement feels right. Trust your instincts when deciding on furniture placement. Your room should 'feel right.'"

—TipsFromTeddi.com

Gut feelings. You know, that gnawing in the pit of your stomach that warns you that you are about to do the absolute stupidest thing you could do? Something that will ruin life as you know it?

I've got one now, standing at the butcher counter in King Kullen, the grocery store in the same strip mall as L.I. Lanes, the bowling alley cum billiard parlor I'm in the process of redecorating for its "Grand Opening."

I realize being in the wrong supermarket probably doesn't sound exactly dire to you, but you aren't the one buying your father a brisket at a store your mother will somehow know isn't Waldbaum's.

And then, June Bayer isn't your mother.

The woman behind the counter has agreed to go into the freezer to find a brisket for me, since there aren't any in the case. There are packages of pork tenderloin, piles of spare ribs and rolls of sausage, but no briskets.

Warning Number Two, right? I should be so out of here.

But, no, I'm still in the same spot when she comes back out, brisketless, her face ashen. She opens her mouth as if she is going to scream, but only a gurgle comes out.

And then she pinballs out from behind the counter, knocking bottles of Peter Luger Steak Sauce to the floor on her way, now hitting the tower of cans at the end of the prepared foods aisle and sending them sprawling, now making her way down the aisle, careening from side to side as she goes.

Finally, from a distance, I hear her shout, "He's deeeeaaaad! Joey's deeeeeaaaad."

My first thought is *You should always trust your gut.*

My second thought is that now, somehow, my mother will know I was in King Kullen. For weeks I will have to hear "What did you expect?" as though whenever you go to King Kullen someone turns up dead. And if the detective investigating the case turns out to be Detective Drew Scoones... well, I'll never hear the end of that from her, either.

She still suspects I murdered the guy who was found dead on my doorstep last Halloween just to get Drew back into my life.

Several people head for the butcher's freezer and I position myself to block them. If there's one thing I've learned from finding people dead—and the guy on my doorstep wasn't the first one—it's that the police get very testy when you mess with their murder scenes.

"You can't go in there until the police get here," I say, stationing myself at the end of the butcher's counter and in front of the Employees Only door, acting as if I'm some sort of authority. "You'll contaminate the evidence if it turns out to be murder."

Shouts and chaos. You'd think I'd know better than to throw the word *murder* around. Cell phones are flipping open and tongues are wagging.

I amend my statement quickly. "Which, of course, it probably isn't. Murder, I mean. People die all the time, and it's not always in hospitals or their own beds, or…" I babble when I'm nervous, and the idea of someone dead on the other side of the freezer door makes me very nervous.

So does the idea of seeing Drew Scoones again. Drew and I have this on-again, off-again sort of thing…that I kind of turned off.

Who knew he'd take it so personally when he tried to get serious and I responded by saying we could talk about *us* tomorrow—and then caught a plane to my parents' condo in Boca the next day? In July. In the middle of a job.

For some crazy reason, he took that to mean that I was avoiding him and the subject of *us*.

That was three months ago. I haven't seen him since.

The manager, who identifies himself and points to his nameplate in case I don't believe him, says he has to go into *his cooler.* "Maybe Joey's not dead," he says. "Maybe he can be saved, and you're letting him die in there. Did you ever think of that?"

In fact, I hadn't. But I had thought that the murderer might try to go back in to make sure his tracks were covered, so I say that I will go in and check.

Which means that the manager and I couple up and go in together while everyone pushes against the doorway to peer in, erasing any chance of finding clean prints on that Employee Only door.

I expect to find carcasses of dead animals hanging from hooks and maybe Joey hanging from one, too. I think it's going to be very creepy and I steel myself, only to find a rather benign series of shelves with large slabs of meat laid out carefully on them, along with boxes and boxes marked simply Chicken.

Nothing scary here, unless you count the body of a middle-aged man with graying hair sprawled faceup on the floor. His eyes are wide-open and unblinking. His shirt is stiff. His pants are stiff. His body is stiff. And his expression, you should forgive the pun—is frozen. Bill-the-manager crosses himself and stands mute while I pronounce the guy dead in a sort of *happy now?* tone.

"We should not be in here," I say, and he nods his head emphatically and helps me push people out of the doorway just in time to hear the police sirens and see the cop cars pull up outside the big store windows.

Bobbie Lyons, my partner in Teddi Bayer Interior Designs—and also my neighbor, my best friend and my private fashion police—and Mark, our carpenter—and my dogsitter, confidant and ego booster—rush in from next door. They beat the cops by a half step and shout out my name. People point in my direction.

After all the publicity that followed the unfortunate incident during which I shot my ex-husband, Rio Gallo, and then the subsequent murder of my first client—which I solved, I might add—it seems like the whole world, or at least all of Long Island, knows who I am.

Mark asks if I'm all right. Did I remember to mention that the man is drop-dead-gorgeous-but-a-decade-too-young-for-me-yet-too-old-for-my-daughter-thank-god? I don't get a chance to answer him because the police are quickly closing in on the store manager and me.

"The woman—" I begin telling the police. Then I have to pause for the manager to fill in her name, which he does: *Fran.*

I continue. "Right. Fran. Fran went into the freezer to get a brisket. A moment later she came out and screamed that Joey was dead. So I'd say she was the one who discovered the body."

"And you are…" the cop asks me. It comes out a bit like who do I *think* I am, rather than who am I, really?

"An innocent bystander," Bobbie, hair perfect, makeup just right, says, carefully placing her body between the cop and me.

"And she was just leaving," Mark adds. They each take one of my arms.

Fran comes into the inner circle surrounding the cops. In case it isn't obvious from the hairnet and bloodstained white apron with Fran embroidered on it, I explain that she was the butcher who was going for the brisket. Mark and Bobbie take that as a signal that I've done my job and they can now get me out of there. They twist around, with me in the middle, as if we're a Rockettes line, until we are facing away from the butcher counter. They've managed to propel me a few steps toward the exit when disaster—in the form of a Mazda RX7 pulling up at the loading curb— strikes.

Mark's grip on my arm tightens like a vise. "Too late," he says.

Bobbie's expletive is unprintable. "Maybe there's a back door," she suggests, but Mark is right. It's too late.

I've laid my eyes on Detective Scoones. And while my gut is trying to warn me that my heart shouldn't go there, regions farther south are melting at just the sight of him.

"Walk," Bobbie orders me.

And I try to. Really.

Walk, I tell my feet. *Just put one foot in front of the other.*

I can do this because I know, in my heart of hearts, that, if Drew Scoones was still interested in me, he'd have gotten in touch with me after I returned from Boca. And he hadn't.

Since he's a detective, Drew doesn't have to wear one of those dark blue Nassau County Police uniforms. Instead, he's got on jeans, a tight-fitting T-shirt and a tweedy sports jacket. If you think that sounds good, you should see him. Chiseled features, cleft chin, brown hair that's naturally a little sandy in the front, a smile that... Well, that doesn't matter. He isn't smiling now.

He walks up to me, tucks his sunglasses into his breast pocket and looks me over from head to toe.

"Well, if it isn't Miss Cut and Run," he says. "Aren't you supposed to be somewhere in Florida or something?" He looks at Mark accusingly, as if he was covering for me when he told Drew I was gone.

"Detective Scoones?" one of the uniforms says. "The stiff's in the cooler and the woman who found him is over there." He jerks his head in Fran's direction.

Drew continues to stare at me.

You know how when you were young, your mother always told you to wear clean underwear in case you were in an accident? And how, a little further on, she told you not to go out in hair rollers because you never knew who you might see—or who might see you? And how now your best friend says she wouldn't be caught dead without makeup and suggests you shouldn't, either?

Okay, today, *finally,* in my overalls and Converse sneakers, I get it.

I brush my hair out of my eyes. "Well, I'm back," I say. As if he hasn't known my exact whereabouts. The man is a detective, for heaven's sake. "Been back awhile."

Bobbie has watched the exchange and apparently decided she's given Drew all the time he deserves. "And we've got work to do, so..." she says, grabbing my arm and giving Drew a little two-fingered wave goodbye.

As I back up a foot or two, the store manager sees his chance and places himself in front of Drew, trying to get his attention. Maybe what makes Drew such a good detective is his ability to focus.

Only what he's focusing on is me.

"Phone broken? Carrier pigeon died?" he asks me, taking in Fran, the manager, the meat counter and that Employees Only door, all without taking his eyes off me.

Mark tries to break the spell. "We've got work to do there, you've got work to do here, Scoones," Mark says to him, gesturing toward next door. "So it's back to the alley for us."

Drew's lip twitches. "You working the alley now?" he says.

"If you'd like to follow me," Bill-the-manager, clearly exasperated, says to Drew—who doesn't respond. It's as if waiting for my answer is all he has to do.

So, fine. "You knew I was back," I say.

The man has known my whereabouts every hour of the day for as long as I've known him. And my mother's not the only one who won't buy that he "just happened" to answer this particular call. In fact, I'm willing to bet my children's lunch money that he's taken every call within ten miles of my home since the day I got back.

And now he's gotten lucky.

"*You* could have called *me*," I say.

"You're the one who said *tomorrow* for our talk and then flew the coop, chickie," he says. "I figured the ball was in your court."

"Detective?" the uniform says. "There's something you ought to see in here."

Drew gives me a look that amounts to *in or out?*

He could be talking about the investigation, or about our relationship.

Bobbie tries to steer me away. Mark's fists are balled. Drew waits me out, knowing I won't be able to resist what might be a murder investigation.

Finally, he turns and heads for the cooler.

And, like a puppy dog, I follow.

Bobbie grabs the back of my shirt and pulls me to a halt.

"I'm just going to show him something," I say, yanking away.

"Yeah," Bobbie says, pointedly looking at the buttons on my blouse. The two at breast level have popped. "That's what I'm afraid of."

HARLEQUIN®

Mediterranean
N I G H T S™

*Glamour, elegance, mystery and revenge
aboard the high seas...*

Coming in August 2007...

THE TYCOON'S SON

*by
award-winning author*

Cindy Kirk

Businessman Theo Catomeris's long-estranged
father is determined to reconnect with his son, so
he hires Trish Melrose to persuade Theo to renew
his contract with Liberty Line. Sailing aboard the
luxurious *Alexandra's Dream* is a rare opportunity for
the single mom to mix business and pleasure. But
an undeniable attraction between Trish and Theo is
distracting her from the task at hand....

REASONS FOR REVENGE

A brand–new provocative miniseries by *USA TODAY* bestselling author **Maureen Child** begins with

SCORNED BY THE BOSS

Jefferson Lyon is a man used to having his own way. He runs his shipping empire from California, and his admin Caitlyn Monroe runs the rest of his world. When Caitlin decides she's had enough and needs new scenery, Jefferson devises a plan to get her back. Jefferson *never* loses, but little does he know that he's in a competition....

Don't miss any of the other titles from the REASONS FOR REVENGE trilogy by *USA TODAY* bestselling author **Maureen Child**.

SCORNED BY THE BOSS #1816
Available August 2007

SEDUCED BY THE RICH MAN #1820
Available September 2007

CAPTURED BY THE BILLIONAIRE #1826
Available October 2007

Only from Silhouette Desire!

REQUEST YOUR FREE BOOKS!

2 FREE NOVELS PLUS 2 FREE GIFTS!

HARLEQUIN®

Blaze®

Red-hot reads!

YES! Please send me 2 FREE Harlequin® Blaze® novels and my 2 FREE gifts. After receiving them, if I don't wish to receive any more books, I can return the shipping statement marked "cancel." If I don't cancel, I will receive 6 brand-new novels every month and be billed just $3.99 per book in the U.S., or $4.47 per book in Canada, plus 25¢ shipping and handling per book and applicable taxes, if any*. That's a savings of at least 15% off the cover price! I understand that accepting the 2 free books and gifts places me under no obligation to buy anything. I can always return a shipment and cancel at any time. Even if I never buy another book from Harlequin, the two free books and gifts are mine to keep forever.

151 HDN EF3W 351 HDN EF3X

Name	(PLEASE PRINT)	
Address		Apt.
City	State/Prov.	Zip/Postal Code

Signature (if under 18, a parent or guardian must sign)

Mail to the **Harlequin Reader Service**®:
IN U.S.A.: P.O. Box 1867, Buffalo, NY 14240-1867
IN CANADA: P.O. Box 609, Fort Erie, Ontario L2A 5X3

Not valid to current Harlequin Blaze subscribers.

Want to try two free books from another line?
Call 1-800-873-8635 or visit www.morefreebooks.com.

* Terms and prices subject to change without notice. NY residents add applicable sales tax. Canadian residents will be charged applicable provincial taxes and GST. This offer is limited to one order per household. All orders subject to approval. Credit or debit balances in a customer's account(s) may be offset by any other outstanding balance owed by or to the customer. Please allow 4 to 6 weeks for delivery.

Your Privacy: Harlequin is committed to protecting your privacy. Our Privacy Policy is available online at www.eHarlequin.com or upon request from the Reader Service. From time to time we make our lists of customers available to reputable firms who may have a product or service of interest to you. If you would prefer we not share your name and address, please check here. ☐

HB07

HARLEQUIN®

Blaze™

COMING NEXT MONTH

#339 HARD AND FAST Lisa Renee Jones
She's been in and out of locker rooms her whole life. Now Amanda Wright is there looking for the inside scoop to take her column to the big leagues. When pitcher Brad Rogers offers a sexy time in exchange for an interview, her libido won't let her refuse!

#340 DOING IRELAND! Kate Hoffmann
Lust in Translation
A spring that inspires instant lust? With the way her life's been going, Claire O'Connor is ready to try anything—even if it means boarding a plane to Ireland. But once she arrives, she knows there has to be *something* to the legend. Because all she had to do was set eyes on gorgeous innkeeper Will Donovan, and she wanted him….

#341 STRIPPED Julie Elizabeth Leto
The Bad Girls Club, Bk. 2
Lilith St. John is a witch—really! And she hasn't been too good lately. (It seems using a spell to make Mac Mancusi totally infatuated with her was a big no-no. Who knew?) But that doesn't mean she deserves to be stripped of her powers. Especially now—when Mac's suddenly back in her life, looking to rekindle the magic…

#342 THE DEFENDER Cara Summers
Tall, Dark…and Dangerously Hot! Bk. 3
Theo Angelis puts the "hot" in "hotshot lawyer," but savvy, sexy Sadie Oliver's simple handshake sets him aflame. Her brother's facing a murder rap, their sister is missing and Sadie is in terrible danger. Her only way to be involved in the case is to pose as a man. But the heat in Theo's eyes never lets her forget she's *all* woman….

#343 PICK ME UP Samantha Hunter
Forbidden Fantasies
Do you have a forbidden fantasy? Lauren Baker does. She's always wondered what it would be like to have sex with a total stranger. And now is the perfect time to indulge. After all, she's packed up her car and is on her way to a new life when she spots a sexy cowboy stranded by the side of the road. How can any girl resist?

#344 UNDERNEATH IT ALL Lori Borrill
Million Dollar Secrets, Bk. 2
Multimillion-dollar lottery winner Nicole Reavis has the world at her feet, but all she wants is hot Atlanta bachelor Devon Bradshaw. The Southern charmer has plenty to offer and plenty to teach Nicole about the finer things…including the route to his bedroom. But she's got a secret to keep!

www.eHarlequin.com

HBCNM0707